S0-ASK-949

WITHDRAWN
Public Library

Swan of Tuonela

Also by Charles Wyatt:

Listening to Mozart [University of Iowa Press, 1995]

Falling Stones: the Spirit Autobiography of S. M. Jones [Texas Review Press, 2002]

Swan of Tuonela

Charles Wyatt

Hanging Loose Press
Brooklyn, New York

Copyright © 2006 by Charles Wyatt

Published by Hanging Loose Press, 231 Wyckoff Street, Brooklyn, NY 11217-2208. All rights reserved. No part of this book may be reproduced without the publisher's written permission, except for brief quotations in reviews. This is a work of fiction; any resemblance to actual events or persons is entirely coincidental.

www.hangingloosepress.com

Printed in the United States of America

10 9 8 7 6 5 4 3 2 1

Hanging Loose Press thanks the Literature Program of the New York State Council on the Arts for a grant in support of the publication of this book.

Acknowledgments: Some of the stories in this collection appeared in slightly different form, in the following publications: "Rembrandt's Nose," "Mona," "John Gardner's Ghost," and "Listening," *Hanging Loose*; "Free Lessons," *Lynx Eye*; "The Wine Press," *Marlboro Review*; "Swan of Tuonela," *Prairie Schooner*; "Weasels," *Boolaboo*; "A Woman's Name, in the Dark," *Chelsea*.

Cover art from Getty Images
Cover design by Marie Carter

Library of Congress Cataloging-in-Publication Data available on request.

ISBN: 1-931236-65-8 (paperback)
ISBN: 1-931236-66-6 (cloth)

Produced at The Print Center, Inc. 225 Varick St., New York, NY 10014, a non-profit facility for literary and arts-related publications. (212) 206-8465

TABLE OF CONTENTS

For Raphael Dannatt

With special thanks to the editors of Hanging Loose; my friends; and readers.

REMBRANDT'S NOSE
Philadelphia, 1975, 2002

I

One thing led to another. I was looking in the back of the closet for an old pair of running shoes to wear in the garden, and I came across two framed drawings that Anna had done of Mary—they don't especially look like any particular person—Anna's style was spare and stylized, and they're just torsos, but they are drawings of a very naked lady—erotic to any viewer, I'd guess. Mary's dead these twenty-five years and Anna—I don't know. Maybe she's still out there, alone and gardening like me. I decided I'd hang the drawings again, and then I dropped one—the glass broke and I cut myself badly trying to clean up. It took only five stitches at the Doc-in-a-Box, but I bled handsomely. Even after my cleanup the carpet looked like a crime scene and the drawing was ruined. I decided against hanging the other. Let's say I can take a hint.

*

Anna and I were living in Philadelphia; it was the early seventies and we lived in two little (make that tiny) three-story houses that were almost back to back in a glorious slum just off South Street. The area is pretty swell now, I understand—an annex of Society Hill—but then it was the refuge of the desperately poor. One house rented for $30 a month, the other $35. The extra five bucks was for sunlight. We lived in the dark one (its front door faced the blank wall of a deserted elementary school at a distance of about five feet), and Anna used the other for her art studio and to store the things she would find on the street and bring home. She couldn't leave any useless object alone on the street, no matter how hopelessly broken or disgustingly soiled. The large pieces of junk went on the first floor of the studio. It always smelled bad—like an outhouse, I insisted. Anna said she liked the way outhouses smelled. The neighbors were noisy and dangerous, and we didn't stand out.

Anna's teaching was mostly in Germantown, at the YWCA, but

she liked this neighborhood because there was a community of people like us who painted and sculpted and had shows in little galleries on South Street. The area had once been a bridal district, but all those stores were gone, moved or disappeared forever; I never thought to ask. Not many of my friends were interested in marriage in those days. We lived together and felt artistic, bohemian. The disapproval of our parents, somewhere in Ohio or Nebraska, was enough to keep us inspired and dedicated to our art. Anna taught two ceramics classes in Germantown, hand-building and wheel throwing. The hand-building class, which she insisted on, was always undersubscribed. The wheel throwing class had a waiting list.

Sometimes she taught painting and drawing in West Philly, at a community center not too far from the University of Pennsylvania. I taught flute and recorder students in Germantown, too; and in any other place I could cobble together a few lessons. For almost a year, I took the Broad Street subway to its last stop, Olney Avenue, at Girls' High, and then the bus for another thirty or forty blocks to teach two students who lived in the same neighborhood—the commute took longer than the lessons. Sometimes I'd get a playing job. I practiced. Anna painted and sold teapots in the little stores on South Street. We got by.

It's not surprising that I had a lot of free time. Anna showed me how to throw pots on the wheel she kept in the basement of the studio, and I made a few teapots that were so ugly and inept they seemed to have character and actually sold. But the work was too messy—and I figured that I might eventually get good at it and then my stuff would become bland and competent. I couldn't bear the thought of being overtaken by competence—I decided I wanted to paint. But it became immediately clear that I couldn't draw. Anna said I could take her drawing class in West Philly. But first I should learn something about drawing.

"You listen to music all the time," she said, as I pulled her hair back over her shoulders. She was stir-frying zucchini and her hair always hung in front of her face. I liked her hair. She hid behind it, but it was pretty—glossy and dark and long enough for me to gather it into a rope against her back. Sometimes she let me braid it. She handed me the wooden spoon.

"Don't let anything burn." In a few minutes she came back from the studio with her book bag.

"Look at these drawings the way you listen. And be careful with it—it's special." She gave me a little book with a rubber band holding the broken bindings. I had been listening to Bach flute sonatas over and over, but mostly, stoned, to stuff like Jefferson Airplane. I wondered if I should get high to look at Anna's little book.

I spread out its pages on the table. Rembrandt drawings. I wasn't surprised that Rembrandt could draw: Camels, lions, beggars, elephants, portraits of wealthy burghers, windmills and farm houses under clumps of trees. I shuffled through the semi-detached pages thinking vaguely of the baseball cards I collected when I was a kid.

"Stop." Anna pinned my hand on a page with a drawing titled "Saskia Sitting Up in Bed."

"Look at the lines around her hands." There was a little nest there where Remmy's pen had been busy. It was a place for Br'er Rabbit to hide. I turned the page upside down. Now there was a different nest. I could tell that Anna approved. I put the little book back together. We ate the stir-fry. Then I spent the rest of the afternoon finding those magical little nests (we were always a little stoned in those days), in the crook of a beggar's arm, the corner of a building, an elephant's tail. I saw the jagged lines a goose quill made and the warm smudging flow of black chalk. Anna hovered but left me alone. It was better than the baseball cards, almost as satisfying as listening to Grace Slick.

That night I went to West Philly with Anna and spent an excruciating hour trying to draw a vase with some weeds in it. I was supposed to look at the weeds, not the page, and to keep my pen in constant contact with my tablet. I was of little faith. I cheated constantly. My weed was soggy, slovenly, and ultimately did not resemble a weed. Anna was as kind to me as she was to her other students. This I found refreshing. She suggested I draw with my left hand—the weeds sneered at me from their table in the center of the room. I undertook to stare them down, pen gripped in left hand, teeth clenched. I began to draw, stranger to myself, to the room—I glared at those things, somehow composed of the stuff lines could represent. And then, when I realized I had been holding my breath, and let the air in (or out, it can't matter)—I had drawn something very like a weed. I was astonished.

At the end of class, I met Mary, who was an old friend of Anna's, from other classes, I supposed. She was taking this class for free in exchange for modeling—I didn't think much about it at the time. Mary had a car, an old Plymouth, and drove us home, across the Schuylkill and down South Street—it turned out she lived in our neighborhood, across Lombard Street from the beer distributor. She and Anna yakked in the front seat and I dozed in the back, still glowing with my recent triumph. Several of my fellow students had commented favorably on my left-handed weed, especially Mary. She was obviously a discerning artist. What were they talking about? Her boyfriend, Stan, wasn't around. He had gotten into trouble with some people he did business with—she was giving up on him. Anna was giving her some new age ballast—I knew Stan. He had sold me some crappy hash. I could never figure out what Mary saw in him.

Some old guys were in a screaming fight at the corner of 4th and South. Mary ran the light. I thought it was probably a good move. A siren behind us but we were cool. We got out and waved. Home. You almost didn't notice the smell—new garbage and something like old basement—the elementary school next door had been boarded up for a thousand years. There were dead animals in it—probably cats. Our neighborhood couldn't support rats. Not many, anyway.

That night Anna asked me if I thought Mary was pretty. I said I guessed she was, and then Anna slipped down under the covers and began to fondle me. After a while I tried to pull her up, but she wouldn't budge. And even afterward, she wouldn't budge, burrowing against me when I tried to tug at her. We fell asleep that way and in the morning when I remembered it, I realized it wasn't the sort of thing we could talk about.

I worked at my drawing every day, and every day I leafed through the little book, even copying some of the drawings, although Anna hadn't suggested I try. There was one called "The Naughty Child" that I tried several times. It's a woman trying to hold on to a toddler who's having a screaming fit. You can see him slipping out of her hands. My toddlers were invertebrates. I did better with landscapes but I couldn't get the trees. In the Rembrandt drawings, they seem to hold the wind. And then there was one special drawing, the "Portrait of Saskia in a Straw Hat." It was inscribed by Rembrandt: "This is drawn after my wife, when she was 21 years old, the third day after our betrothal, the 8th of June 1633." Saskia is wistful and lovely, with her left hand lightly touching the side of her face, elbow resting on the table where she is sitting, flowers twined around the crown of the hat and in her other hand.

The portrait was silverpoint on white prepared vellum and was sold at auction, along with most of his other possessions, by the Insolvency Court in 1656. I read about it in one of Anna's big art books. The guy had gone broke—he could have been one of our South Street neighbors. He had seen the same kind of shit my neighbors had. But Saskia at twenty-one hadn't seen shit yet. She wasn't a worker like Anna. At least in the drawings. He drew her gazing out a window or in bed with a toothache. You don't ever see her pushing a broom. She was from a wealthy family and when she died, things got complicated. I was just beginning to see that the life you plan doesn't always work out. Mozart had been buried in a pauper's grave—I read about that, too.

*

Two more classes in West Philly and I was beginning to swagger home with my portfolio. I even had some fanciful self-portraits which made me look like a Picasso character—but make no mistake, I still couldn't draw. It was before the fourth class, the one after the self-portrait exercise, when Anna said we'd be drawing from life. We were riding the streetcar and it was noisy and crowded and I didn't ask what that meant. When class started, Mary came out of a side room wearing a robe, walked to a chair in the center of the room and then dropped the robe. We were going to draw Mary naked.

I couldn't get over my instinct to avert my eyes and for a while my drawing involved elaborate preparation of the wash and a general splashing and spilling and dropping of pens and brushes and other essential and nonessential articles. After a while curiosity took over. Mary was very smooth and her skin glowed pink. Anna had once observed to me that old people are much more interesting to draw because of their wrinkles and folds. Mary could assume many interesting positions, however. She was very flexible and resourceful. She didn't seem to mind all those eyes on her. I knew I had blushed when she dropped the robe, and I soon discovered I couldn't draw her. I couldn't even get an outline. And I was aroused. It was awful. Anna didn't say anything when she glanced at my procrastinations.

Perhaps she thought I had converted to abstraction.

On the way home, in Mary's car, the two chatted about ordinary things, the clay supply at Germantown where Mary was also newly involved, teaching a yoga class.

"How did it go, James, drawing from the model?" Anna asked me this as if Mary weren't driving the car.

I couldn't think of a suitable reply—something about the Emperor's new clothes?

"Was it hard?" Mary asked, and then giggled.

Anna reached back and stroked my leg, and for the rest of the drive, nobody had anything else to say. At least there weren't any fistfights on South Street that night. Mary waved to us when she let us out at South American Street. She *was* a pretty girl. Anna burrowed her nose into my armpit as I was unlocking the door. I knew what was going to happen when we got to bed.

I woke up about three a.m. and went to the bathroom on the top floor, carefully climbing back down the spiral stairs—they weren't level and on more than one occasion had pitched me into the bedroom. Down in the kitchen I brewed tea. Mice rustled in the walls. There was one which seemed to live in the little gas range, dodging about the burners, only taking a powder when we cooked. There were no sounds louder than the ticking clock. Anna had left some of her art books on the kitchen table. Rembrandt's nudes didn't seem especially erotic to me—they were too Dutch, too overly plump. Mary was not plump.

I flipped the pages to the self-portraits. He would dress up for them in turbans or funny hats, but he was painting himself honestly as he aged. At the end, his nose had become a potato. I climbed back up to the bathroom so I could look in the mirror—I was wide awake, but Anna seemed to be sleeping soundly. I looked myself in the eyes until there was a stranger across from me in the little room. I could imagine him aging—his nose would be easier to draw when it became misshapen. And the wrinkles would supply character.

After Saskia died, Rembrandt took up with his child's nurse, Geertje Dircx, a bugler's widow. But six or seven years later, he decided he liked his housekeeper, Hendrickje Stoffels, better. Geertje made trouble. Rembrandt had her committed. See it all in the sad eyes, the sagging nose. I took myself to bed and closed my eyes. I would draw my self-portrait with closed eyes, I decided. Mine or the portrait's, I wasn't sure.

*

The next morning Anna went to Germantown. I had the day off until some students came by in the late afternoon. I was restless. By ten o'clock, I was in front of the beer distributor's building, dodging insouciant forklift drivers. Looking up to the second-story window across the street, I saw someone beckoning to me. It was Mary. She had to come down to let me in—buzzer technology hadn't reached Lombard Street in those days.

She didn't say anything, just turned and walked up the stairs, giving me the one camera angle I didn't need. But perhaps there were others.

"You want a cup of tea?"

"Sure."

"Would you rather smoke a joint?"

"I'm easy."

We ended up having both. Ginseng tea and a joint already rolled that tasted like hash. Just a couple of dainty tokes before Mary put it out. I have recorded here all we said, leaving out the ambient kitchen noises involving cups and spoons, turning the water tap and the like. When Mary had taken the last toke, and carefully extinguished the joint, she walked over to me, and, taking my face in her two hands, drew me to her and expelled the smoke into my mouth. I figured out what she was doing eventually (dope makes you patient), and inhaled some of the last of it. Then I caught her and kissed her. The rest was very nice, a little exuberant, but nothing broke, and then we might have dozed a little, there on the floor, among our clothes, in patches of late morning light. After a while, I dressed and, feeling a bit at a loss and a little stoned, sat down at the table where we had had our tea. Mary still lay on the floor, stretching occasionally, relaxed, but not smiling.

"Do you want to draw me now?" she asked.

I did. I really wanted to draw—there was something I already imagined I could feel, something languid and wonderful. What happened then was that Mary got me a large tablet and some chalk and settled herself back artfully into the pose which had inspired me, and I worked with the chalk industriously—then found her drawing pens and India ink—and after more time than it had taken us to make love, I stopped. It was noon and the street was quieter because the guys with the forklifts were having lunch. My drawing was awful. Stoned or not, I still couldn't draw—this was just busier than the rest.

"Let me see it." She got up and began to dress.

"Don't do that," I almost said, but I caught myself. I felt as if I had said it, and that now I shouldn't watch her. But she was graceful doing it, and I told myself it was something I'd likely never see again. Eventually she looked over my shoulder at my drawing—which at the moment seemed to me a fine likeness of a plate of spaghetti.

"That's wonderful," she said, her hands on my shoulders, staring at the carnage I had made with my own hands. I felt like the five-year-old who has learned to draw a house with a chimney and a squiggle of smoke.

"Would you like to have it?" I asked.

She smiled, in just the way I imagined the girl smiles in the lyrics of the Rolling Stones song we listened to in those days. I put the tablet on the table and then backed toward the door. My mouth had gone dry.

"Well, then," I finally managed.

I had lost something—the moment, my composure. I'm sure my hands were shaking. Ginseng and hashish. Given the same thing today, I'd probably fall into a coma. I backed down the stairs as if I were leaving a sleeping child. I could feel connections breaking, seasons changing. Mary called something out that I didn't hear. I had to stop on the stairs so she could say it again: "You go home now."

"What?" I said. I was halfway down the stairs and couldn't see her—I was beneath the surface of the sea.

"Home," she said, and she said it in a strange way, as if it were a question. It was as if she had just heard that word for the first time, and wasn't sure what it meant. I thought she might come to the top of the stairs, and I waited for a while before I left.

The key was in the deadbolt and I had to leave the door unlocked behind me.

The street was bright and hot—not summer hot, but hot like the metal of mufflers and tail pipes. It was too hot for the alley to smell bad. I could see the guys with the forklifts, but I couldn't seem to hear anything. I walked the block home reluctantly, my feet shuffling. I had decided I wanted my drawing. I wanted to go back, but I couldn't. It might never have happened.

FREE LESSONS
Philadelphia, 1974

It is going to be a long summer. June in South Philadelphia is already uncomfortably hot. Even the noise of the trucks around the warehouses is hot. The boards closing the doors and windows of the organ factory next to James and Anna's alley are hot. The nails that hold them in place. The weeds growing in lots where old buildings have been razed are taking heart. The ailanthus trees gather themselves to spring. James has been reading Hermann Hesse—*Steppenwolf* and *Magister Ludi*. In his damp basement, rows of pink fluorescent lights hang over tender young cannabis plants. He has decided that teaching is indeed a noble calling, perhaps the most noble of them all. He has put handbills along the best two blocks of South Street. Free Flute Lessons, they proclaim. There is one in the window of the Painted Bride Gallery where James sometimes performs. There is one on the wall next to the City Delicatessen. He has even gone up two blocks to the hardware store, but he's never seen anybody reading the posters there—some are years out of date.

Back in the little house on Alley Row, James waits for his phone to ring. Will Tommy scare them off? Tommy hasn't bothered his paying students, but James hasn't taught in the summertime before. Now that it is warm, Tommy hangs out his window, it seems, for most of the daylight hours. Tommy's window is over his own front door, but Tommy lives next door to James. Standing in front of his own stoop, James can reach up and hand Tommy a beer. He has done this more than once to shut him up.

Tommy is an orator and a philosopher. That the subject of his exploring mind is the white man and that his quest for metaphor involves wrenching profanity can't be avoided. In Tommy's lexicon, Whitey has earned his place. If metaphor is the discovery of resemblance, Tommy, hanging out his own window, each day, beginning in the late morning when a rancid slice of sun from Lombard Street begins to make its way into the narrow alleyway— Tommy is the Cortez, the Magellan of such discovery, James thinks. Fortunately, it's nearly impossible to understand his mumbling. It seems to consist mostly of an extensive taxonomy of excrement in both rest and motion—Tommy's tongue and lips work like a whittler's knife around a language too hard, too rigid and class-bound—Tommy softens it, mumbles it, nearly makes it into music. One can only occasionally understand the words—they crop up in patches, like the dog droppings on the street, smeared sometimes by careless heel-marks. But his meaning—his meaning as he hangs out the window in a tattered brown shirt, yellow eyes flecked with red, lips alternately dry and puffed or dripping—Tommy's meaning is clear enough. James can imagine his new students turning away in legions.

"I had it all planned," James complains to Anna, who is drying the coffee cups. "I was going to teach them to improvise, even little kids, and then we'd play one weekend at the Painted Bride. It's been a week and nobody's called. Is it because it's free?" James busies himself with getting the last good toke out of a joint that someone has left on the stove top. He coughs professionally and raises his eyebrows to Anna, who shakes her head. Anna's hands are red from working on the wheel in the basement. She puts the cups on a shelf. She has made most of them herself.

"I'm going to Germantown today. Why don't you come? You can play with clay while I teach. It's free, too."

There is a loud sound of something breaking, more than one plate, likely, from Tommy's side of the kitchen. The walls are brick but the mortar is crumbling. On the third floor, the bricks themselves have fallen away a few feet under the roof.

"I feel like we live in a stall," James says to himself, since Anna has gone down to the basement and is making purposeful rummaging noises.

"My mother used to say you get what you pay for," James pitches his voice to carry down the spiral staircase. "Do you think that's what's going on?"

"Everybody's mother says that." Anna's still in the basement, wrestling bags of clay.

"Mother fucker!" A woman's voice, but deep. This is Elsie, who lives with Tommy.

"Mother *fucker!*" The accent has moved majestically and there is the sound of more crockery breaking.

*

18

James has left Anna in Germantown to teach her evening class. The alley is quiet as he unlocks the door, but there are grinding noises coming from the beer distributor down Lombard Street. The phone is ringing.

"Hi, this is Fred. I'm calling about the free lessons?"

"Fred?" It is a girl's voice.

"Yeah, Fred, my name is Fred. You don't want to know what Fred is short for and I don't want to tell you. I think I remember you from the Painted Bride. Didn't you play one time with those two guitar players?"

James sits down. He realizes that Elsie is singing up on the top floor. He really likes to listen to her sing—but it means that there is going to be more angry noise soon. Singing, shouting, breaking, and then, with any luck, unconsciousness. The welfare checks must have come in.

Fred is talking about some co-op in West Philly where she and her friends do something for the disadvantaged.

"So why free lessons? Oh, I'll bet you want to return something to the community, right? Or maybe you just want to hit on young girls. I'm a lesbian, you know."

James wonders if he could ask Elsie to sing "Amazing Grace." Probably not.

"What about guitar lessons? I'd really rather have guitar lessons."

"I'm just giving flute lessons—you have to have a flute and you might have to buy some music."

"Oh I've got a flute. I played in high school, but I thought this was going to be free."

"Maybe flute lessons aren't really what you want to do. I'd want you to practice every day, at least a half hour."

"I'll bet. You know, I'm not really a lesbian. Can I come over to your place now?"

*

James meets Fred at the corner of American and Lombard streets. The singing has stopped and the shouting has begun. Joe, the guy in the house on the other side of Tommy's has shouted up at them from the alley, and Elsie has thrown a brick at him. James figures the police are likely to show up. Sometimes when he gets mad, Joe will light a fire in his kitchen and call the fire department. Joe is a little wiry guy who lived with his mother until she had a heart attack or stroke around Christmas time. He had been really quiet before she died.

Fred drives a Jeep and has a black and white dog with one standing ear. The dog's name is Willy and he smiles at James from the passenger seat. Fred has short brown hair and fine features. So does Willy. James asks Fred if she will meet him at the Painted Bride up South Street. It's clear he isn't going to be able to teach at home. Maybe the guys will let him teach in the gallery. He hasn't thought to ask.

Jerry doesn't like the idea at all, but Frank does very much. Frank doesn't want the dog in the gallery, but Jerry wants to draw the dog. Two old men in Hawaiian shirts. This was Anna's title for their last show. It wasn't bad. Frank is the tall one. Jerry is nearly a hunchback. They bicker only slightly less than Tommy and Elsie. James discovers that Fred's flute is unplayable and she accuses him of trying to rip her off with a flute repair scam. Jerry announces that free lessons at the Bride is a great idea, but only after Fred and Willy have switched out the door.

On the way back to the alley, James goes to an open lot and starts pushing at the bricks and paving stones in it. There was rain earlier in the day and it's still steamy. Sometimes there's a floating crap game across the street but it's quiet now. James has got a jar and he's catching the huge roaches that run out from under the bricks. Most of them get away but he's got five or six. They race around in the jar, shitting and breaking off each other's legs. When he gets back to the alley, there are neither police cruisers nor skeins of fire hose—the altercation between Joe and Elsie must be in remission. James opens the end of a hutch-like contraption along one of the stripped brick walls of his kitchen. It's full of cedar shavings and there is a green lump, a large green lump in its shadows. He pours in the roaches and the lump transforms itself into a large toad, about the size of a bullfrog. It hops once toward the scattering roaches, then spits its tongue at them violently. In a few seconds they have all disappeared and the creature is visibly swallowing. Its eyes close rapturously as it does so.

"Toad!" James croons to it.

There is a knock at the door. This is Fred again.

"Willy's in the Jeep. I got a little hot with those two weird guys going on about letting him in and drawing him and keeping him out. What's that thing?"

"That's Big Toad. She came from Arizona in a half gallon ice cream container."

"How do you know she's a she?"

"I don't really. She's never sung."

"What do they sound like when they sing?"

"I've got one loose in the basement that sounds like a bullfrog. Regular old garden toads trill. Sound like canaries. Like that."

There's a yellow bird hopping in a cage by the sink which emits a short trill as if on cue. The cage is shaped like a haystack. Anna has welded it. James can picture her in her welder's helmet.

"Would you fix my flute?"

James gets his bag of tools and takes the flute apart while Fred sits on the bottom steps of the spiral staircase. Fred is wearing bib overalls with holes in the knees. Her white knees are exposed and are nice to look at, James thinks as he looks up from his work.

"Don't you want to bring Willy in and maybe give him some water?"

Fred brings in the dog. After lapping some water in one of Anna's bowls, Willy sniffs at Big Toad's hutch.

From inside the hutch there's a sound, something like a loud fart.

"Big Toad, did you do that?" James has left his work and peers into the hutch.

He is startled when he feels Fred pressing herself against him.

"Hello," she says.

"Flute lessons," he says.

"My mother used to say," Fred says, pushing her hands up under James' shirt, "that you get what you pay for."

*

By the end of June, James has five students. One is thirteen, a girl he taught at the Settlement School. One is George, a guy in his fifties who seems to live in different places on South Street. Another is a friend of Anna's from Germantown, a woman who might be George's age but who seems to be well-to-do.

"Why would she want free lessons?" James asks Anna.

"Probably for the same reason you want to give them. She got really excited about it when I mentioned that you were trying to get students. She thinks it's spiritually uplifting."

Her name is Chase. She buys the music James suggests on the phone and shows up at the Bride with a silver Haynes flute which she has bought for the occasion. She has paid top dollar for it, too.

"This is such an interesting place for a music lesson," Chase bubbles. James has had to wait for her to circle the gallery. The show is Jerry's, who does house portraits in crayon. He follows her, rubbing his hands together. She's likely to buy. And she does at the end of the lesson. Three of them—one the size of a door. Jerry gets $200 in cash and James gets a promise that she will practice *every* day. She has hoot owl inflections. James isn't sure whether she is putting him on. Anna tells him that Chase is eccentric.

George can play already, but he uses all the wrong fingerings. James asks him if he would like to learn the correct fingerings and he smiles benignly.

"Perhaps these are correct for me? How would we know?" George has a full frosty beard and wise eyes (Anna says he has wise eyes— James isn't sure what the hell wise eyes look like). George makes pretty good money teaching Zen or dealing dope or selling antiques to the likes of Chase. James figures he is going to learn some deep shit if he can avoid pissing George off, so he suggests they play long tones together. George seems to like this, and James does too, he can get some practicing done. George's lessons soon involve no talking at all. James wonders if the deep shit he is learning may be too deep for him to appreciate.

The thirteen-year-old, Sarah, has been on lesson five of the Rubank Elementary Method for the past six weeks. With Sarah, the greater danger is that she might practice. When she takes that into her head, she will distort rhythms, invent new fingerings, and begin to play in the wrong octave. Sarah is charming, enthusiastic, and a little in love with James. She tells James about her week, her friends, her pets at home. Sometimes she is actually unable to produce a sound and James must show her how to begin. She is always delighted with this. Nothing discourages her. James feels that Sarah may be the perfect student. He has come to enjoy her lessons most of all.

Fred's lessons are infrequent and never at the Bride. Fred believes you get what you pay for and tends to show up with Willy, unannounced. Fred does know Anna's teaching schedule, however.

The fifth student is Frank. After lurking at one of James' sessions with George, Frank produces an open G sharp antique which is black with tarnish. When James offers to clean it for him, he declines. Shiny flutes have no character. Frank is shy around George, waits for him to leave.

"Remember that time you played last spring and everybody got up and left? You should have called that *Lessons*. See, it's a focus, a theme. *Lessons*. It sounded like what you and George just did. You've got to find the frame and then the world will buy it. Now, how do you make a sound on this thing?"

"You got to hold it on the right, Frank."

Frank likes to argue, but he's not bad. He just gets nervous around George, or if anybody comes into the gallery. James wants him to improvise but he likes *40 Little Pieces for Beginner Flutists*. Minuets. Frank is working on a suite of drawings he calls *Minuets*. *Minuets* is a frame, Frank says. He's getting inside minuets.

In late July, Anna says she's going to spend two weeks with her friends Dianne and Jim who raise goats and ganja in western Pennsylvania. She says to James he's got that much time to lose the free flute students. Especially Fred. James knows she's right. He'll have a graduation. They'll all play at the Bride. Frank owes him.

It's not exactly a concert. Frank and Jerry have a show opening, so there's a bowl of punch and James asks Chase if she'll come and play but she's going to be out of town—she buys two more of Jerry's crayons and drives off in her Land Rover—no more lessons, dear, she bubbles to James, who wonders what she's going to do with that flute. So that leaves Frank who can't improvise and won't play if George shows, and George, who might come, and might play but is too deep to say, and then Sarah's family is going on vacation. Sarah leaves her lesson in tears because she has been making up new pieces with titles like "Running Squirrels" and "Robins Watching for Worms." James promises her he will play at least one of her songs himself. Fred says she'll come and bring her friends from the co-op.

Night of the opening there are plenty of South Street types milling around because Jerry and Frank go way back. Nobody goes as far back as Jerry and Frank except George, who is pointedly not present. Fred, who had earlier stopped by the alley and shared some astonishingly powerful hashish with James, is present, but Willy is nowhere to be seen. James sees two musicians he knows, Alan, a French horn player, and Simon, the clarinetist from the opera. They are talking to Jerry, probably interested in booking a performance—a lot of musicians come down here to play. James waves but they don't seem to notice him. There are actually a lot of people crowding into the Bride now. James has decided that he's just going to start playing and see what happens. Will people get quiet and listen or will they just keep schmoozing and he'll be background? He imagines that he doesn't care. He's been thinking about a blues scale that he's going to use to make something slow with wide intervals and a lot of space. There's a place in the back of the gallery where the sound is good and there's a little raised platform.

James starts to play: He's using a rising figure that takes the space of one breath, then he's pausing for about the space of two long breaths, then he plays it, or something like it, again. It seems to have the effect of a kind of placid fanfare on the milling people. Some of them sit down on the chairs that are arranged in one section of the gallery, others get quiet. James begins to fill in all that breathing space, pleased to have listeners—he feels stoned but not fucked-up stoned.

This is when James notices George and the black guy that's with him. Charles used to live a few doors down from James and if he hasn't hocked it . . . James can see it now. He's brought his bass clarinet. Pretty soon George has got his flute out and he's playing along and then Charles begins to play. Someone dims the lights and James flashes on "Sonny's Blues." But Charles is no blues man. He bites down on the reed and cracks the sound into as many shards as physics can bear. Charles has never learned any fingerings—he just wiggles and twitches his fingers as fast as he can. Charles is strong and has good wind. James knows from personal experience that he can go on like this for at least an hour. Most of the sound is squeaks but occasionally a low note will pop out, producing an astonishing incongruity. George is already in a groove, playing long notes, looking as if he's someplace else.

James backs into the darkness and packs up his instrument. Someone, probably Jerry, has focused a spot on the band, which is growing now, because both Fred and Frank (who has overcome his fear of George, apparently) are joining in. Frank is playing minuets. James can see that Fred is playing, but he can't hear it. He can see she's puffing her cheeks. Charles is beginning to lose speed with his fingers, but the squeaking and honking is getting stronger. It's like a locomotive with locked wheels, James thinks.

How long has this taken? A minute, two? The audience is captivated, no, stunned—no one is moving to escape as James slips out the front door—if there were restive murmurs, they would have gone unheard.

South Street is a bass solo. It's not silence so much as something missing. There's no focus. A few passers-by. Bus fumes and garbage. James could swear he can hear a nighthawk overhead but it's bound to be an artifact, something expiring in his inner ear. He notices Willy tied to a parking meter. Scratches his ear.

"That your dog?" A Walter Brennan voice. James looks around, still on his haunches. This is George. No. Not George, but what a resemblance. The guy is smiling and maybe he was a hockey player once.

"Do I know you?" Willy actually bares his teeth at the guy.

Splinters of bass clarinet and flute waft from the closed door of the Bride.

"What the hell is that?"

"It's a concert, an event—do you know George? You sure as hell look like him."

"He's my father." The guy laughs. He's got hardly any teeth and the smell coming from him is worse than South Street.

The door to the Bride opens and several people come out, more or less in a rush. Fred is in the lead. She grabs up Willy, gives James a peck on the cheek, wrinkles her nose at Walter Brennan, and flounces off. Now the door to the Bride has been propped open and people are pouring out. You can still hear the bass clarinet, but there's a lot of shouting coming from inside.

"Your lady friend?" says the guy with an indefinable inflection. James feels himself blushing.

The guy shakes his head. "You're never going to see her again."

"Call the police," somebody shouts from inside.

"They have free eats at these things?" the guy asks James.

"Sure, go on in, and say hello to George." James is standing in the street now because of the milling people. He can't see where Fred and Willy have gone. Maybe Walter Brennan is right. A blue police cruiser pulls up and James has to work his way into the crowd to get out of the way. The bass clarinet has stopped and James can hear Jerry yelling, his voice cracking with frustration. The police are talking into their radios, providing narrative calm. Sonny's gone out to sea, James thinks. He sees Tweedle George and Tweedle Walter Brennan, arm in arm. "Magic Theater," George calls out to him and winks. Walter's got the stiff leg limp down pat. James is stoned, he remembers. There's a cop on a horse now and James walks with a group of people up in the direction of the hardware store. He can see more police cruisers. "Who's going to pay for this?" This is the last voice he can make out, one of the old men in Hawaiian shirts. As he turns to walk toward Society Hill, he remembers he forgot to play "Robins Watching for Worms."

*

"Mother Fucker." Tommy's staring at the bricks. What he's saying is mantra, words forced out with the strength it takes to haul a mattress up a narrow staircase.

"Mother Fucker."

"Yo, Tommy," James says.

Tommy gives something back, after significant silence, a bit like a hum, the working noises inside a transformer, perhaps.

Snakes, James thinks, suddenly having trouble focusing.

"Charles playing his bass clarinet up at the Bride." Tommy's looking at James like Big Toad looks at a roach.

"I think he's done. I came from there. He did pretty much what he used to do around here."

"You call the police?"

"Nope. Somebody did, though. You call 'em? I thought you and Charles were tight."

"Charles is an asshole and he owes me money."

There's another siren, but it's a fire engine. The thing goes right by the alley and James has to wait for it to pass the intersection.

"You ever see snakes, like here, here in the alley?

"Mother Fucker." This with resignation. It's dark inside Tommy's window and James can't see him well. Everything is slow and quiet again. James has got his hand on his own doorknob and is turned to look at Tommy, who hardly moves. The street ambiance is filtered, cars moving by, the siren two blocks away now. The doorknob is a little loose in its workings, but very smooth against his palm.

"No snakes, huh?" James has got his key, and Tommy's laughing to himself. This is the laugh of a man who knows snakes, James thinks.

"Tommy." James can't see him in the window space. "Charles told me to tell you he has the money he owes you. I'll bet you could still catch him."

In a minute, Tommy hustles out his door. He's bent over but he moves fast. He's very agile for a man his age. He's got a cap on, an old-fashioned cap the like of which James has only seen in movies. He's mumbling something to himself, but James can't hear it.

He was in such a hurry he didn't close the door. James can hear Elsie singing up on the third floor. She doesn't sound like she could move as fast as Tommy.

James lets himself in the door. The room is dark but it's just like his own kitchen. He just wants to look out the window, anyway.

And there it is. The alley. Tommy's alley. And look at those snakes.

"Mother Fucker," James says.

"Elsie!" he calls up the stairs. The singing stops.

"Your door was open. Want me to shut it for you?"

"You get out of my kitchen. Who is that down there?"

"It's James."

"Go on then. You go home."

"There's snakes out there, Elsie."

"Get your white ass out of my kitchen or my black ass is coming down these stairs with a brick."

James steps out into the alley and shuts the door. Now he notices there aren't any snakes.

A dog barks. Elsie begins to sing again. James has almost got it figured out, what she's singing, but she pauses in her singing as if to listen for something. Her window opens.

"You get inside now," she says. Her voice is quiet, tired, not entirely unkind.

His little kitchen smells like the bacon he made for lunch. There is a sudden thump and scrabble from the toad hutch. The bird startles and hops on its perch, making it ring against the wires of the cage.

James turns out the light, then peers out his window at the alley. This is about the time of night when Charles used to play that bass clarinet. James thinks that it wasn't all that bad. He just needed some lessons. There's a streetlight at the end of the alley, usually, but tonight it didn't come on. Maybe somebody broke it. It's too dark to see anything more. It's late at night and there aren't any snakes. Tommy's key scratches in the lock next door and James can hear the two of them talking, their lowered voices. In a minute he'll go to bed. Just now, he's going to sit for a while in the dark of his kitchen.

THE WINEPRESS
Philadelphia 1973, 1999

"James, what are you smoking?" Anna has come up from the basement to find James nodding at the kitchen table with a book in his lap. The room is cloudy and there's a bad smell, not the sweet smell of cannabis, but dirty woodsmoke. *Joseph and his Brothers* falls to the floor.

"It's Joe again."

They rush out the front door, out the alley to the street, and around to the other side of the building where James begins pounding on a door similar to their own.

"Joe, what's on fire?" Joe!" There is a scrambling sound from inside while James continues to pound on the door with the flat of his hand.

"What, what, what?" Joe has opened the door and is standing there in his undershirt and shorts. He is very bowlegged. It is difficult to tell whether he is more hairy or dirty. The room behind him is dark, but a cloud of vile-smelling smoke drifts out into the walkway.

"Do you still have a fire?" Anna pitches her voice like the schoolteacher she sometimes is.

"What, what, what?" Joe turns around and peers into the dark and smoky room.

"I was taking a little nap, okay? A little nap."

"Joe, is it out?"

"No fire, no fire."

"Joe, this is the second time this week"

"No problem, I pissed on it."

"Joe."

"I'm sorry. I fell asleep. It's out, it's out. Go away. I gotta pee." He backs into the room and slams the door.

Anna and James walk back to the street. "He's wrecked."

"You want to call the police?"

"Yeah, right."

"Maybe we should move to Germantown." Anna pours out two cups of tea while James works the front door like a bellows. "You're just bringing the outside smoke inside. Sit down. James, have some tea and stop playing with the door."

"I don't want to move to Germantown. I want to have Joe killed."

"And then some other junkie will move into that place and set fires. It's an old building. *You* practically exploded the water heater last month."

The sound of a bass clarinet squeaking covers James' response. It is very loud and comes from a short distance down the alley. James closes the door.

"Well, Charles is back. Maybe it's just this building. Look, I'll work it out. I'll push Joe in the door when Charles is beating his wife and Charles will dispatch him with the bass clarinet, destroying the instrument in his efficiency. Then the police will take Charles away."

"And they'll take one look at the building and have us all evicted."

"So you can move to Germantown." James picks up *Joseph and his Brothers* from the floor. "You know, I really like this neighborhood. Maybe we could just find a place that isn't quite so colorful. Not that there's anything wrong with our neighbors. I think midnight clarinet concerts go very nicely with smoke inhalation. Are you ready?"

Anna assumes an inscrutable expression and, while Charles mixes squeaks, quacks, and crescendos, James begins to read aloud:

"Of sin in the sense of an offence to God and His expressed will we can scarcely speak in this connection, especially when we consider the peculiar immediacy of God's relation with being which sprang from this mingling of soul and matter: this human being of whom the angels were unmistakably and with good reason jealous from the very first."

Anna raises her teacup but discovers it is empty. She looks with longing toward the kettle.

*

"This is the block. Look how neat the houses are. No beer distributors, no furniture warehouse. Look at those scrubbed stoops." (Jerry and Frank at the gallery have told James and Anna about their neighbors, an old Italian couple, who have decided to put their house up for sale.)

At the door Anna takes James' arm and stops. "It's a sunny neighborhood, and it doesn't smell bad."

"Then why are you squeezing my arm? I feel like I did when I went door to door on Boy Scout paper drives."

Anna lets go of James' arm, smoothes his sleeve, denim, a baggy overshirt which he bought from an Amish mail order catalogue. It has snaps, not buttons. Before Anna can put her finger on the doorbell, the door opens and a plump white-haired woman gathers them into the house. The effect on James is like the time a flock of pigeons descended on him while he was talking to a friend in Rittenhouse Square. His friend had been feeding them breadcrumbs. More wings and more pigeons than he had ever seen in one place. He felt as if he were rising into them. Mrs. Mecoli is shaking his hand. Inside the house is dark, the glare of the sun still erasing detail. She actually speaks to her husband in Italian.

They are making the tour. James will hate himself for how little he remembers of moments like this in his life. It is not the room itself which is dark but the furniture in it, which seems to be staggering under the weight of what Anna likes to call, without irony, "pretty things." There is a corner populated by figures of pigs. The more James looks, the more pigs there are, and they have been collected without regard for their mutual proportions. They are like sparrow and elephant and their effect (in glass, ceramic, wood, metal, and perhaps papier mache) is more macabre than whimsical, although James thinks before wrenching away his gaze that neither impression was probably intended. There is one (should he look back?) standing on its hind legs playing a flute while others dance.

There are glass-fronted cases that seem to brim with glassware, goblets and cruets arm in arm with ordinary tumblers and what even seem to be small mason jars, competing for space with painted plates and awkward teapots. There is a crucifix on every wall and, in the darkest corner, the family photos mix formality of pose with the effect of crowding one might expect in an old person's icebox. There is a small television with rabbit ears resting like a child's coffin on a carefully draped table.

Mrs. Mecoli and Anna have made some cosmic connection and are chattering rapidly. Is it English? James forces himself to concentrate. It is, surely, but, stranger than a language he doesn't understand, Anna is asking the old lady questions about something (he thinks it might be lace) he has never heard her discuss. They have left him alone on the staircase with his hand trailing behind. The old man, very grizzled and fierce, is standing at the foot of the stairs and he waves at James as if he were a wasp.

"Go. Go," he says roughly. James turns, feeling as if he has let a ground ball go between his legs with the bases loaded.

Upstairs there are two bedrooms, which James is reluctant to enter—he is willing only to poke his head across the threshold. He sees a mirror that does not seem to reflect and another crucifix, perhaps larger than downstairs. There are more photos, some of them standing in arrangements like the pigs below. Mrs. Mecoli sweeps him into the bathroom and he is instructed to turn on the water. He does this, on and off, and there is a loud complaining shriek from the pipes or even the water heater, and Mrs. Mecoli is eloquent in explanation.

As they return to the parlor and then to the kitchen, Anna tells Mrs. Mecoli about how James turned up the water heater and forgot, allowing steam to get in the cold water pipes, causing their toilet to explode when James flushed it in the middle of the night. They are standing in the kitchen and the old man is frowning as Anna elaborates on the water rushing down the spiral staircase of their little house. Mrs. Mecoli bursts into Italian and provides what apparently is the translation because old Mecoli bursts into laughter and begins pounding James on the back.

"You must see basement," he roars, and leads the procession down a set of sturdy but un-railed steps. The basement walls, constructed of irregular stones, serve as the house's foundation. The cement floors are swept and immaculate. Old Mecoli gestures to the stairs. "No waterfall. *Secco.*" He makes wiggling fingers of falling water between bouts of mirth and appears keen for more back pounding, but James has maneuvered himself out of reach.

"Dry?" James offers.

"*Secco*, yes, dry, dry, dry." The old man is delighted and practically dances a jig.

"What is that thing?" Anna asks pointing to a kind of barrel-shaped object in the corner. It is circular, made of some kind of hardwood slats darkened with age, and at the top is a heavy iron screw mechanism.

Mrs Mecoli speaks rapidly to the old man who replies at some length. Then he frowns at James and Anna.

"It is for the . . . for the vino. Old in the family. Not for sale." Mr. Mecoli rubs his hands and this is somehow a signal for them all to troop back up the stairs to the kitchen. Mrs. Mecoli shows James and Anna the tiny back yard with its neat vegetable garden.

"You will have coffee before you go?" While there is a rising inflection in the old man's voice, the ceremony does not seem to be optional. Anna is given a delicate cup, but James has a heavy white mug.

"For the man." Mr. Mecoli pours a heavy dollop of whiskey into James' coffee and the same into his own. The coffee and liquor seem to James to have the taste of tree bark and earth, dark and inky. He drinks it down and they leave amidst much handshaking. The old man seems to be able to speak more English at the end of their visit than at the beginning. He is as warm as the whiskey.

That night the phone rings and Anna picks up. James doesn't like the telephone, never has. Anna has students who call her about glazes. James tunes her out: *Hell is for the pure; that is the law of the moral world. For it is for sinners, and one can sin only against one's purity. If one is like the beasts of the field one cannot sin, one knows no hell. Thus it is arranged, and hell is quite certainly inhabited only by the better sort*—James will put this on the refrigerator, next to Harry's calling card: *Destroy good and bad, right and wrong, ugly and beautiful, great and inferior, all value, moral and ethical judgments. There is no good or bad in reality, so refuse to take part in its usage. Follow this path and you walk in absolute peace. This is the way of Zen. ZEN Wa 5 6663.* Harry is Anna's welding teacher. James hasn't seen him in the last six weeks and the word is around that he is in jail.

Anna says it was Mrs. Mecoli, that they're going to throw in the winepress with the house and that they've come down on the price. James was afraid that was what the call was about. On a whim, he tries Harry's number. There is no answer.

Their second visit to the house ends with the same coffee laced with whiskey. James has managed to enter the bedrooms and to look in a few closets. He notices that the pigs have been carefully dusted. He asks about Angelo Mecoli, the opera second flutist who tried to cover the pages of James' music during a solo, hoping to screw him up. The old man is dismissive. Angelo might or might not be a relative of his. What does it matter? Actually, Simon Edwards, the clarinet player, has told James that Angelo is from this part of South Philly. Anna and Mrs. Mecoli spend much time in the back yard while James and old Mecoli sit with their coffee and whiskey. James declines the offer of a refill. Two whiskeys before noon? Mr. Mecoli has taken out the winepress and worked the turnscrew to show it is ready to make the vino. Like the hatch on a submarine, James thinks.

This phone call comes later in the evening, a time when Anna's mother might call (Anna does seem mostly to be listening). *"Buttercup, house wren, mud lark, buck rabbit, old frog, old mouldwarp, swamp beaver, little buckbat."* James is reading in *Joseph and his Brothers* about Huia and Tuia who are very old and figure in a scene in Potiphar's garden. These are some of the endearments they have for each other. For some reason, James has underlined them. One of the old Egyptians is blind and the other can scarcely hold up his head. Forget they are brother and sister, parents of a child they have made a eunuch. Old age is old age. James wonders about the old Italian couple and their life together. Where have they come from? Where will they go? He thinks about the winepress—in his and Anna's house, there would be a winepress and a potter's wheel. Perhaps there would also be a loom. He wonders if he and Anna will grow old together. He realizes he has no pet name for her. If he made up a name, she would pinch him.

*

James is talking to Anna in a largely empty room. There are folding chairs for a few dozen people, and a small podium. Thirty years have passed. They haven't seen each other in the past ten.

The occasion is the memorial service for a friend. Harold was a composer when James first knew him, then a painter—they had been students together. The first time James introduced Anna to Harold, she splashed him with milk from a half-gallon container. Anna was volatile in those days. Now she's holding a cane because of a serious automobile accident in the past year, but James thinks she looks like the old Anna.

And like the old Anna, she's talking just under the level of ambient sound. James hears "milk carton" and knows she's talking about that day when she first met Harold. It was Harold she splashed, but might it have been James she was angry with? What had he done? James can't remember. A careless remark about a woman's place, perhaps. Harold had handled it all gracefully, and the two had become the best of friends. Now he's gone. James takes Anna's hand but quickly lets it go. He'll tell some of his Harold stories to the assembled and then play the flute piece Harold wrote for him. Anna will sit quietly. Afterward he'll ask her to write and she'll give him a patient smile.

The phone call had not been Anna's mother, but Mrs. Mecoli again. The reason they were selling the house so cheaply was that burglars had broken in, not once, but three times. The neighborhood was terrible. The burglars had stolen everything of value. The Mecoli's had never used the winepress, which they bought from a neighbor. They could not sell the house to Anna and James, whom they regarded as their children.

Listening to Anna and her inaudible story about the milk carton, James thinks about Harold, their old neighborhood, the pig collection at the Mecoli house. He and Anna could have made wine together. They had talked about it that night. Before the phone call. Then someone says that it's time for the ceremony to begin.

James is playing Harold's flute piece. While this is a background effect, it's important to notice that the quality of the performance is rough—that James is out of practice and that Harold's piece is somewhat lugubrious. The gathered friends, however, are all listening raptly. Whatever it is they are hearing, it takes them to important places in their lives. One is sitting in a rowboat, silently watching swallows circling above in last light. Another has become a child, chasing fireflies. Anna can see the priceless expression on Harold's face as the milk drips down from his nose. Even she can't remember why she splashed him. A young singer who will be performing several of Harold's songs is thinking about the repeats she has agreed with her accompanist not to take.

The music never quite fades but we're no longer in the hall. We're moving about the city, disembodied—we see scrubbed stone steps scooped with wear, boarded and broken windows, ailanthus-studded lots, the very weeds seeming to wilt under the sun's inching onslaught, the Delaware and the Schuylkill, hypnotic, authentic, nursing coils of iridescence in eddies and, in the open basement of a burned-out house, something like a blackened handle with a threaded shaft, necessary artifact, almost hidden in a clump of thistles. See the bees, drawn to the pale blue flowers at the top of the thistles. The stalks move in the wind and the bees orbit around them. This is when we realize that we can hear nothing, that now even the thistles are gone, and that some story must be over.

MONA
Vermont, Nashville, Philadelphia 1978

James had seen the old man work this theme before. He was playing possum, leaning over in his chair as if he were asleep, his chin touching his chest. The student, who seemed to be beyond simple terror, had stopped fumbling with the tuning slide of her flute, and had begun addressing the gathered masterclass as if it were her job to give a lecture, rather than play a melody and then accept criticism. Because the melody was the "Meditation from *Thais*," she had decided to describe the plot of the opera. James could tell what was coming because he could see old Sauvage's hands tightening their grip on the arms of his chair.

They were in a large room that had been temporarily converted from an artist's studio so the old man could meet with his students. Several oversize paintings in progress had been hung high on the walls to get them out of the way. James felt he knew them too well, that he knew most of these people too well, who were sitting, all of them, in exactly the same places, the places they had taken nearly two weeks ago. The largest of the paintings was directly behind the teacher and his student. It was a reclining female form that had probably been transferred from a photograph. It was unfinished—a face and an outline. When the old man got out of his chair, it formed his background. There was something impatient about it, James thought, but patience was not the key to what had been going on here.

Sauvage would teach three or four hours at a time, and the students volunteered eagerly, hoping to be the one he would treat kindly, the one whose promise he would recognize. But this had not been a season for praise. The old man would listen impassively while the student played through the entire piece, growing progressively more and more nervous. Then the carnage would begin, as it was about to begin here. James moved his folding chair noiselessly another foot toward the back wall and the sliding door. He had slipped away before. He would walk for a while, smelling the ferns and pine trees. Summer was a beautiful season in Vermont. Now Sauvage was asking the woman why she was not playing her piece. He had spat out "merde," not "shit," which indicated he was already over the line, and the woman had yet to play a note.

Then there was a banging and scraping at the sliding door behind James—a group of about four people. James decided instantly that any distraction would be useful. He rose and worked the recalcitrant door open while holding a finger to his lips. He had managed only to open the door a few feet, so it was necessary for the party to file past him one by one. With his attention still on the front of the room, he was only vaguely aware of passing bodies, and of a faint perfume that struggled briefly before it was subsumed in the prevailing atmosphere of wood smoke and pine. There was much restrained confusion counterpointed by Sauvage, who continued to berate the student at the other end of the room.

The last in the procession was a tall dark-haired young woman with high cheekbones. She had already passed to the row of chairs in front of James when she spun and stage whispered, "James!" He looked at her again. Immediately he remembered himself sitting on the spiral stairway of his little house in Philadelphia, listening to a student, this student, playing a Bach sonata. He could hear her awkward phrasing, even in dissonant counterpoint to the "Meditation," which had at last begun in the front of the room. Then as suddenly it was gone and he was grasping her hand and making a show to silence any more whispering. She was beaming, genuinely glad to see him, repeatedly turning and smiling, then putting her finger to her lips in recognition of the old man who now had risen from his chair and was circling his student like a wolf after caribou.

What was her name? Mona. That was it. Mona had taken lessons for almost a year, and then her father had been killed in an automobile accident, or might it have been a plane crash. . . . She used to complain about her love life, give him long soulful looks, grasp his arm, everything but bat her eyes. During the lessons, he had taken to sitting on the staircase to get away from her.

Sauvage was shouting now—he had started the routine he went into about his teacher, Emil Verhey, how he had taken an oath never to disappoint him—and the woman was in tears. "Lunch break," an authoritative voice declaimed, and Sauvage was led out of the room, still fuming. The *Thais* woman was surrounded by a sympathetic crowd.

Mona introduced James to her husband, Tom. Tom was in a hurry to get back to Philadelphia and only took time to comment that it was ironic that musicians would pay so much to receive abuse. James wondered distractedly whether his students, whether Mona, had sought him out because he seldom gave praise. But this was a new Mona, she was lovely, still touching everyone around her, but with enthusiasm rather than neediness. James asked her to have lunch with him. It seemed perfectly natural even though the husband had just stepped out the sliding door and the woman in the front row was still weeping.

In the restaurant, James watched her. He liked the license this situation gave him: He could look all he wanted, yet he saw little he could remember later—dark skin, very smooth and, against the light, sometimes a fine down, prominent cheekbones. Her vivacity—perhaps that was it, she was always moving—was disconcerting.

She seemed larger than he had remembered. Without the flute in her hands she was a presence. He mused, remembering her breathy tone, the monotonous phrasing.

"What are you thinking about?" Mona was still chewing, but the way her attention bounded from one thing to another, like a distracted puppy, was really charming.

"Do you remember my little house in Philadelphia? I used to sit halfway up the spiral staircase when you played for your lessons. I was just remembering you, how beautiful you looked." James wasn't lying. He had thought she was pretty. He had to work hard to keep from making her cry in the lessons. Now she beamed, then blushed.

"Well, you're not my student anymore. I can compliment you." James said, beginning to feel foolish.

"You never complimented my flute playing."

James felt restored. She had granted him the powers of a teacher and he wondered what he might do with them as he watched her, a little flustered, turn her attention to her salad.

"I was lonely in those days." James couldn't resist another foray. "It wasn't easy to watch you, to keep Bach the subject of conversation."

Now she seemed thoughtful, and James wondered if he had gone too far. But she began to chatter about her life, flagging only when she came to the end of her salad. James offered a story about an outdoor concert at the end of his orchestra season. There were hatching mayflies all over the music. An F at one moment became G in the next as the notes crawled up the scale. Deep breaths were hazardous. Mona laughed, but remained distracted.

He saw her several times that week during the master classes, and once he asked her if she was planning to play. She shook her head—she was an auditor. She knew what that old man would say to her. James already had. There was going to be a party on the last night of the session. Was he going?

James took her to the party which was oddly quiet, perhaps because of the guitarist who was playing almost formal sets. James knew him and they talked about playing a new and difficult piece for flute and guitar which both of them had heard of, but had not performed. James knew it would come to nothing. The guitarist had some good dope. Everybody was complaining about the old man.

James lost track of Mona and the party became noisier. He saw his friend Phil leaving with a blonde girl who played the French horn—Phil winked at James across the room. James had met Phil two years before—they had played a Demerssman *Fantasy on William Tell* for the old man, variations for flute and oboe—it had been a triumph. Sauvage had told stories and danced and made jokes. The piece had reminded him of his youth. Afterward, Phil and James had drunk Pernod with him. Those were different days. They had caroused, but there was music to be made, and Sauvage still cared.

Then Mona was at his elbow, asking him if he would take her home. It was late. The apartment where she was staying was long and narrow and there was a bicycle practically blocking the hallway. Behind the bicycle, the room was dark, and before Mona could reach a lamp, James took her in his arms. He felt stoned and remembered that she had smoked, too. How much, he wondered? She was warm and they kissed for a long time standing in the room behind the bicycle. James began to push her toward the back of the room where the bed must certainly be, but she wouldn't move. She was a tall girl. They kissed again. James told her he wanted to make love to her. She shook her head, but it wasn't that she was saying no. She just kept shaking her head.

"It wouldn't be right. Tom. It's Tom's birthday."

Then she kissed him again and he couldn't think very clearly, because this was a more passionate kiss than the first, which had been merely long and quiet. This was like high school. Tom's birthday. He tried to slow her down. He kissed her eyes.

"Let's make love."

"It wouldn't be right." More tongue thrusting and lip nibbling.

He tried to move her toward the back of the room but she wouldn't budge. She was strong.

"Mona. Think about me sitting on that spiral staircase and you playing. No one knows what that moment was like. It is a secret between us. No one will ever know about this night. No one. It will be something you and I can share and always treasure."

And he kissed her again and moved slightly toward the back of the room. This time, sighing deeply, she budged. It was dark, and James was stoned and, he realized, half drunk. I'm not even going to remember this, he thought, as he maneuvered her, almost slow dancing, to the bed. I feel like a tugboat, he thought.

"Birthday," Mona said, almost cheerfully, as she settled herself beneath him. Her voice seemed to come from another part of the room, as if there were a parrot cage on the dresser.

The next day James leaned his head against the passenger side window of Phil's car. The glass felt cold against his aching head. They were driving to Philadelphia.

"Big night?" Phil asked. He had been humming to himself.

"I met an old student of mine—she couldn't decide whether to get friendly until about three in the morning."

"You always were a poor campaigner. Like McClellan. Never enough troops, never enough supplies. Wait, wait, wait. I, on the other hand, am the Stonewall Jackson of love. Flank attack. My musket was smoking before you . . . "

"Enough with the Civil War."

"Did you have a good time?"

"I hope so."

"You ignored my date last night—not speaking?

"I guess you could say that. She called me a few months ago—she was in town for an audition."

"Did you see her?"

"Nope."

"Were you in love with her?"

"Why would you say that?"

"Because you walked out of my room last summer."

"Did you ever consider that I didn't want to watch you getting a blowjob?"

"She was going to give you one, too."

"She did."

"There. Someday you're going to look back at all of this and realize how small-minded you were. Still are, probably. James, James, wake up."

James had left his car with Anna in Philadelphia and driven with Phil to Vermont. Now he watched Phil peel away from the curb on South Street, waving. The neighborhood was still noisy and dirty, the sidewalks blocked with trucks loading and unloading. Cardboard and packing materials had spilled out of a doorway and James had to walk in the street. Phil had gotten him into mischief often enough. Mischief. He had let that girl spend the night in his room. What would Phil have done? Would he have driven her home? James couldn't think of her name, but she *had* called him once. She liked him. He had pretended he was busy.

Anna was still teaching in North Philadelphia. She let James use her studio when he was in town. They would talk for hours, drinking herb tea. Sometimes James would ask her to come to Nashville with him. Anna would smile and tell him she was happy. And he would tell her that he was not. And she would tell him that he was happy being unhappy. James could see his car locked in the back yard, apparently whole. He would spend the night, catch up on sleep and drive the next morning.

He decided to pick up the ringing phone. Anna didn't have a machine. It was Mona. James felt he was in a crowded room and that the nameless blonde girl was jostling him. He could see her clearly in some kind of summer dress. She had talked to him that night about something, the summers she spent with her family, her sisters—after she had come up to his room from Phil's. But there was nothing around him but piles of boxes and furniture. Anna's apartment had become too cluttered to move around in.

Mona was in Boston. Was he going to be in Philadelphia long? She'd be coming home in a few days. She was talking fast. He must have given her this number. What had he been thinking? He was writing down her number. She had several numbers. He must call her from Nashville. What had happened to the secret they were going to treasure? The phone felt hot against his ear. Her feverish voice. She missed him. The room was dusty and some of the boxes were piled up higher than his head. She seemed almost in tears.

"Mona," James said.

Her voice receded from the room where it had been chasing among the boxes and retreated into the telephone receiver, becoming faint, dwindling.

"Mona," James said. "I love you."

"Thank you," she said.

*

Anna did not come home that evening, and James left for Nashville without the talk he had been looking forward to. He had a folded piece of notepaper in his pocket, covered with phone numbers and elaborate instructions.

Road cuts, corn fields, wheat fields, circling and wheeling flights of blackbirds, starlings probably, crows patrolling the roadside and, hidden behind the rushing envelope of wind and tires, small meadow birds giving their drawn-out calls, repeated phrases, lists, not the endless Tourette's lists of mockingbirds, but little lists, sequences, repeated notes that could almost be out of Mozart, songs for a wide horizon, where the light is yellow, and the crickets are like ground fog—James knew it was all there. Some of it he could see, but he had to hear the rest. He took an exit and pulled over to the roadside.

His back and legs were cramped from driving, but the sharp weed smell made him breathe deeply. There was a steep pitch from the roadside down to a field that had been only partially mowed. The sweet smell came from the cut weeds. He could see a rabbit working its way along the border. There were sulfur yellow butterflies and Queen Ann's lace and there were tall weeds which were blue or perhaps purple—James had a mild case of red-green color blindness. It occurred to him that he could remember making love to Mona. It was exactly what he had told her—a moment he could remember at a time like this.

When he was a child he had kept his arrowheads (there were only two or three) in a cigar box. The cigar box was carefully wrapped in a blanket. He would unwrap the blanket and open the box when he wanted to look at his arrowheads. The box had a faint smell, not of tobacco, but musty, like an old book. The arrowheads themselves were hard and cold and had no smell. Then he would put them back in the box, wrap it in the blanket and put it back on the top shelf of his closet. Mona had a smell that the weeds reminded him of. It was time to put her away, he thought. He picked up a rock and threw it down toward the mowed field. The rabbit at the margin of the weeds disappeared into a patch of Queen Ann's lace and milkweed. It moved deliberately, almost painfully.

*

In Nashville the orchestra's rehearsals had begun, but there was nothing especially interesting on the programs. The old hall had been painted a remarkably ugly gray. James wondered if only he saw colors this way. No one else seemed to mind. He was preoccupied with a solo concert he had scheduled at the college where he taught. November, a good time for a concert, early in the season before people have grown tired of music, before he had grown tired of music. He would play Greek folk songs on a large bamboo flute he had made himself. Japanese shakuhachi music, a North Indian piece. A selection of Renaissance dances for instruments ranging from bass flute to piccolo.

The final piece was to be a Bach violin sonata he had transcribed. He could not decide whether to play it on alto flute. If he did, the transposition of the alto flute would allow the music to sound in the original key. If he played it on his C flute, however, it would be louder, more brilliant. One of the movements was a fugue. He had to arpeggiate the chords. Perhaps it was ridiculous, but he could hear them. But perhaps he was only imagining he heard the chords; probably no one else would. But on the other hand, even the violin did not play *all* those notes at the same time.

He wondered what old Sauvage would have thought. He would have insisted James play one of the Bach flute sonatas, probably the B minor, his favorite. Understand this first, he would have said. I have spent my lifetime playing this piece. Why are you playing violin music? He had said something like that to the woman who played the "Meditation from *Thais*," also a violin piece. Of course, Sauvage often asked his students to play it. Then he would ask them in indignation why they wanted to play it. They wanted to please him. What did he want? He would say the same thing if you played Bach or Mozart or "The Carnival of Venice," James mused as he followed Mona's arcane instructions. Let one number ring once, then call the second.

44

He called her every few days and listened to her talk about Tom. It was not especially difficult for him. He listened and agreed occasionally. It was not much different from the flute lessons: She played the music and he listened, sitting on the third or fourth step of the tiny spiral staircase. After he learned that his suggestions would be difficult for her to follow and that her subsequent efforts would make her cry, he had stopped making suggestions. Her hair was glossy and black and hung nearly to her waist—but the flute was such an effort for her.

He thought it was touching. It should have been annoying. Why shouldn't she call him at his apartment? It was ridiculous. No. He must call her. It wouldn't be right for her to call him. And so he called and half-listened and his mind wandered. He had agreed to a visit. He had four days. He could fly. He'd have to bring his flute for practicing. It would be the week before his program. Mona had made arrangements. A friend was loaning her a town house. She was giving Tom some excuse. They would have the weekend alone together. James had agreed to this as if it really weren't going to happen. He expected her to back out. She was merely exercising her imagination.

*

James pours himself a cup of coffee. There's a knock at the door. It's time for Mona. She's all bundled up with a music bag and a fat case cover for her flute made out of something that looks like carpet. James backs over to the spiral staircase to make room for her. This is a tiny room but she can put her things on the table by the door and James has already put a music stand where he wants it. She's been shopping and has a big bag she sets down by the door. James can tell she wants to talk about it, but he's thinking about the Bach sonata. He wants to hear it again. Musically, it's too difficult for her, but she should be able to play the notes this time, he thinks. Maybe she'll notice something after a while. She claims she's out of breath, but he waves her on. Let's play the B Minor Sonata, he says.

She fumbles with her music, then plays a few notes, warming the flute. They are, James thinks, feeble, incomplete. Annoying, like stifled sneezes. Why doesn't she want to make a wholesome sound? Perhaps her flute is leaking. I could check the pads. No, that would waste the whole lesson. The sonata, then. Yes, play. Play! An eighth note pickup—eighth note on the beat, repeated quarter note. He lets her play the first page. Then back to the first phrase. Pickup. The tonic. B in the middle of the staff. Fingered with the thumb and first finger of the left hand. A note that plays itself. Slurring up a fifth to an F sharp, top line of the staff. All the left hand fingers and the fourth finger of the right hand. This note is fuzzy. Sounds like the word effsharp. Effsharp, effsharp. Hairy air, a leaking tire. Perhaps the flute too high, too low on the lip? Upbeat slurs to downbeat. Bright and easy to soft and muddy. No, not like stepping in something nasty. Play the second note like the first, the first more like the second. Here. James plays the two notes himself, two, three, four times. Now I'll play, you'll play. I'll play, you'll play. And in rhythm. Not just looking around. Like a pump at a well. Or a waterfall. Think of the way the water moves, but seems to pause, motion and rest all at the same time. No, then don't imagine it. Don't look at anything. Listen. Feel the rhythm. Nothing else. Here, I'll count. Be ready. No, let's do it again. So many times you forget what you are doing. Then it will begin to work. Mona! He sees she is crying. He doesn't comfort her. It's her business to recover herself, blow her nose, wipe her eyes. He tells her it is the energy he's trying to help her with. He sighs and asks her what else she's got to play.

*

Philadelphia: An odd thing to be a visitor in a place where he had lived so long with Anna, and Anna still so much a presence here. James pulled his suitcase from the baggage carousel and looked around him again. He didn't see anyone he recognized. Perhaps Mona had sent a friend. She had begun to sound paranoid about Tom, but had insisted that James come when he suggested he could stay home instead and benefit from the practice time. Then there was this woman standing close to him. People didn't do things like that unless they were simple-minded. Mona. She had cut her hair.

"You cut your hair," James said stupidly. Then she began to babble and James felt he knew her, even if he couldn't recognize the way she looked. On the way to the car he tried to imagine what she had looked like before this, but he couldn't. She was too real.

He was going to make love to her, he reminded himself.

There was a feather in the bedroom. A long feather, and lotions, a row of bottles like a barbershop, and a vibrator, no, two vibrators, all arranged conspicuously on the dresser top. Mona said her friend wanted for her to have a special time. James told her that tool use was beyond him. He kissed her and undressed her. He thought that he had flown nearly a thousand miles to see a woman naked. And that he knew what he would see. He rubbed his cheek against her belly and kissed her breasts. He had known and he hadn't known. Some day he would be an old man like Sauvage, he thought, and no young girl would show herself to him.

He'd like to look some more. He'd like to stare at her, at her soft brown skin and her wide hips and long legs and her small breasts, but it would be unkind. He did what she expected him to do, and then they were close, too close to see. They were sealed in a private embrace, and each of them could feel the other in the most selfish way. He'd have liked to experience her feelings and hers alone, and he willed his own away, but they were too strong. Later they made love again and then again. He searched her eyes. He watched her mouth. Her eyes closed. Her mouth told him something, but he couldn't read it. If he kissed her, she would cover him with babbling kisses. Lies and secrets. But he couldn't tell which was which. When she slept he looked at her; but without the hunger, he couldn't see what he wanted to see.

When it came back, and they reached for each other again, he thought he'd finally see, but discovered he couldn't bear to look at her nakedness. Then when they were making love, she began to look at him. He thought her eyes would close, but they did not. And there was a moment in their struggle when he thought he could finally see, but his own feelings surged over him and he must have cried out. He could remember her eyes, and they seemed the eyes of some wild dumb creature, and he was sure he was seeing deep inside of her, and he felt ashamed of her nakedness, and of his own, but then his body was exhausted and she lay on top of him—he couldn't remember how that had happened, and she was gasping and crying. Tears and sweat, he thought. Lies and secrets. A babbling stream of running water, cascading over rocks, speaking a continuous, endless, meaningless utterance. Then she slid to his side and began to breathe deeply, releasing an occasional snore. It was a warm day, but James pulled the cover over them.

He had to get out of this apartment and walk, but she wouldn't go with him. Someone would recognize her. People knew her in this neighborhood. She had to stay inside. It was a warm day in late October. There were a few maple trees in this neighborhood still holding on to their leaves, and the ones remaining were not perfectly golden, like the ones carpeting the sidewalks, but a rusty brown. The city had corrupted them. Bus fume gold, James thought. He knew he was going to walk until he got to Anna's place.

This time she was home—she said she had been reading. There was one room left in her warren with a few chairs and tables. The remaining space had been converted to warehouse her supplies.

"She has feathers?" Anna was more interested than James had imagined.

"I think it's like a sleepover. She has a husband who neglects her and an indignant, vengeful girlfriend. I am Tarzan, husband's just deserts."

There was a throw pillow next to James' chair. Anna applied herself to it in some yogic ordering of her limbs that, while peaceful enough, seemed to take several minutes of careful arrangement.

"What is she, then?"

"Who? Oh, Mona. She's not who I thought. For that matter, neither am I. It's as if I'm trying to draw her, maybe." James looked up at Anna's drawings of her friend Mary, which marched across the wall.

"And you would draw anyone?" Anna asked.

"*You* would draw anything with interesting lines. This is a metaphor and metaphors break down. I'm sleeping with this woman, and all I can think about is looking at her. She's got an outside that I can see, but not much of an inside, I'm ashamed to say. It makes me tired to think of going back."

"You have to look until you get it right." Mary presented herself from many angles along the wall. Poor Mary.

"I'll never get it right. I want to hide under the covers with you."

Anna took his hand. "The leaves. When the leaves are falling. You always used to get this way."

That evening James and Mona watched television.

"Why don't you practice your flute?" she asked him.

"I don't know. I feel more like watching crocodiles. Notice the way they slip into the water without disturbing it."

"Please. I'll let you do anything you want afterward." She batted her eyelashes.

James played his Bach violin sonata transcription, and when he had finished, Mona was sleeping. He turned on the TV again and watched without sound.

*

Nashville, a week later: The lights in the hall are dimmed and then cut completely. There is nothing but the sound of the chairs creaking as the audience moves uncomfortably, waiting. James begins to play. This is the large bamboo flute he made himself. To him it sounds like a mourning dove. He is playing a melody he has derived from a Greek folk song. It is full of fourths and fifths, hollow intervals. The flute sound is hollow. The dark hall is a hollow emptied of light. When James has finished and the light comes up, the audience fills the room with the sound of hands—the stutter of applause. James is in his performance trance. He hears what he is going to play before he plays it, and he thinks, of what . . . ? Of going into a field and applauding. It is like summer nights, he thinks, all those tree crickets. They are afraid to stop, afraid of what music might come next.

Later he's playing the Bach transcription. Twenty-five minutes of design. Like stones in a wall, he thinks. Or an arch. Distribution of force. Patterns, molecules, the true, the miraculous, the tired, the predictable—moonlight is predictable. B minor. He played the B minor flute sonata once for Sauvage. Years before in New York City at auditions for the Marlboro Music Festival. A man came running down the aisle from the dark seats of the hall and vaulted to the stage. "Play that again," he demanded, "All of it. From the beginning." James had thought he was playing an audition—but this was a flute lesson. A man so full of energy he danced.

This was the Sauvage for whom he would play so many times. This was the Sauvage who two years ago—when they had played the Demerssman *Fantasy*, and after many glasses of Pernod—had sung that very same Bach sonata for him and Phil, the Sauvage who always called James "Wood Flute" because of his choice of instruments and who once, in a large masterclass, took the headjoint of his own instrument and banged it against the brick wall to produce a resonant metallic clang: "Can you do that, Mr. James Wood Flute?" and cackled like a crone at the horrified audience.

The night of the Pernod, after Phil left, Sauvage had gone on to Beethoven. He had sung passages from the flute part of the *Pastoral Symphony*, illustrating a narrative that James (partly because he was drunk, and partly because of Sauvage's impenetrable accent) couldn't follow at all. Sauvage was singing to James, and all the while gripping his hand earnestly. James had felt exalted. And now, so old—"Why are you playing this?"

James finishes the movement. Breathes deeply. The audience is silent. Listening or asleep. Now the slow movement. Why do I play this, he thinks. Mona attempted that B minor flute sonata in her first lesson. The one with a passage Sauvage called a hurdy-gurdy. James played it for her over and over. See, Mona, how the handle turns. This is how Sauvage played it for me. Turn the handle. See how it comes back? How everything repeats? She played it slowly, unevenly. Odd to be thinking about this. I'll be an old man and ask them why they play. Perhaps they'll come to me. They will play. I will ask. Odd. What did she think I would want to do? Whatever I wanted. Last movement. See them sitting up. Show them we're coming to the stable. Whatever I wanted. I wanted to be a stranger. Someone who slipped out the door in the cold damp early morning pretending I didn't see her watching me.

JOHN GARDNER'S GHOST
Binghamton, NY, 1999

for Milton Kessler

Beginnings. In debt, divorced. Who isn't? No, it's not that kind of story. The car has got a good 20,000 miles left on it, and it doesn't show a dent, just an ugly scrap of the bright red parking ticket from the last job, impossible to remove—James is still trying to forget that one, giving flute lessons to the militantly unmusical. "Where does it say in the syllabus we have to practice scales?" Now James, having written a book in the spare time his life as a musician always seemed to afford him, is considered a writer. And he will teach fiction writing at Binghamton University. Exposition is material which is out of position. It must come before the story. Except for Perry Mason, of course. But where is the story? Oh, he'll ask this question, not so much of his students, but of himself. My questions are not rhetorical, he'll say. I don't know the answers. Some of them will think he's being subtle. Some will wonder if he's a rube. None will believe him.

He has made his way through Virginia and Pennsylvania, having begun in those horizontal states below. He has stopped and pondered the colorless and sodden vista of Wilkes-Barre where he once played the fabulous flute solo in the scherzo of Mendelssohn's *Midsummer Night's Dream* incidental music without a rehearsal, and for the first time, but not to international acclaim. This material, he decides, is accidental, and thus does not belong in any proper exposition—even if Harold (whose story this must be, at least in part) was there, thirty years ago, driving them all back to Philadelphia where they were students at music schools both lofty and otherwise. Perhaps there's not going to be a story at all, he thinks, just this backing up, like a frog burying itself in mud. Some toads live buried in the ground practically the whole year, waiting for a certain season of rain.

He's in Binghamton now, where the same river he saw in Wilkes-Barre has found the low place between these tired mountains, having made its way almost as digressively as some stories. But now it's time to get down to business: James drives through the campus. The sky has cleared and the day has become sunny and windy. Still, the buildings don't seem to have any color—there's a high rise which subsequently turns out to be the library building. Fake carillon music is coming from speakers at the top. "Beautiful Dreamer." At least this will shoulder out those Mendelssohn chords. James has had them stuck in his head ever since Wilkes-Barre. They were intended to announce the coming of the fairies and sprites of Oberon's magic kingdom, not to spin randomly in mental whirlpools and eddies.

The fake bells from the tower are quaintly out of tune, and if the form of the song is aaba, there is no b. Already James regrets the passing of the Mendelssohn. There are enormous parking lots which seem to have been draped on the hillsides, and the usual mix of grass, dry fountains, and construction. And now there are students, perhaps brought out by the sun, moving energetically about, crowding the walkways, calling cheerfully to each other. James will learn in time that the circular drive through the campus forms the shape of a brain, a feature not in evidence to the first-time visitor, nor to anyone on the ground—he will be reminded often that it is considered a remarkable thing about the university; that and the fact that half a generation before, John Gardner taught in the English department.

Now James must cross the river to find the neighborhood where he has rented a house—when he gets settled he can call Harold, who's back in Philadelphia. Harold had had a piece on the program that night in Wilkes-Barre, but just for strings, and there was a bass player named Randy who lit his farts in the back seat, producing a long blue tongue of flame amid an atmosphere of hilarity and amazement; and Cooper and Larry, two string players from Curtis, hugging the doors and begging for mercy. James had been impressed mostly by the contortionist's posture Randy had assumed for proper ignition. Harold said that music could be almost as entertaining as lighting farts, that he'd write James a flute piece some day, something as magical as the Mendelssohn, he could count on it. And then Harold had rolled down the window, and as skeins of sweet cannabis smoke twined profusely out into the Pennsylvania night, asked the turnpike ticket lady how long it would take to get to Philadelphia if they drove 100 miles an hour.

After passing an overgrown but still elegant cemetery, carefully following his map, James turns left on Beethoven Street (the locals pronounce the "th" after the American manner, he has been told by his landlord)—then right on Lincoln Avenue. He is in a neighborhood of older homes, 70 to 80 years old, he guesses, and built to a formula. Three stories, relatively close to the street, but each with a carefully tended lawn. The roofs are peaked and remind him of the houses he first learned to draw as a child. They tend to exaggerate the vertical. When he steps out of his car and stretches his legs (number 40 is on the high side of the street), he is welcomed by crows, a hollow commentary.

Gordon, the graduate student who is the caretaker of his house, in a special arrangement with the landlord, was supposed to have left a key under the mat for him. James hoists a bag up the steps to the porch. As he reaches the top step, he upsets an aluminum pie pan which is resting on the flat porch rail, spilling what seems hundreds of cigarette butts onto the yard below. Most of them have been smoked down to the filter. James remembers the instructions he has been given by the professor who is renting him this house. There will be absolutely no smoking. Gordon, the caretaker, has been a student of his and is a quiet lad who neither smokes nor drinks. Leaning against the far porch railing are three large garbage bags filled with beer cans. One has broken open and its contents have rolled across half of the porch. There is no key under the mat, but the door is unlocked.

"Welcome to the home of Mickelsson's ghosts," says a coffee-stained note on the kitchen table. There is an embarrassing drawing of a gnome, signed Gordo. And there, stacked on the table, must be his reading. The Gardner novel, and beneath it, *Lord Jim*, and *The Hobbit*. A wonder he has time to draw, James thinks. The house is mostly unfurnished—there are several similar gnome-drawings tacked to the walls, and there is a tilting mobile made of beer cans.

While James is policing the cigarette spill, he notices the house next door seems to have shining objects embedded in its lawn. Squinting his eyes, he can make out brass tubing, trumpets, cornets, French horns, various antique musical instruments half buried in the lawn after the manner of plaster flamingoes. Later that evening he sees lights in the windows, a table with candles set out, real candles, flickering, but no sign of the inhabitants.

*

James meets with his graduate workshop the next evening. They are, he notes sadly, mostly involved with hopeless novels, encouraged cynically by another visiting writer like himself, now safely departed.

Still, he is pleased that they are able to entertain themselves. They love talking about their work and do so relentlessly. Incredibly, a student in camouflage fatigues named Alex is working on a story he calls "Orphans of the Opera." Its characters are not Yniold and Hop Hop, the ones James remembers from Harold's unfinished play of the same name. This is about something else entirely, musical theater it seems; perhaps it is even a coming-out document—there seems to be gay sex—and it is all single spaced and in a number 10 font.

James suggests that readers must be imagined as having free will, that they have been known to put down (and not take up again) a story devoid of punctuation and (seemingly) of verbs—but he is lured into digression by the students, who are surprised he is or was a musician. James tells them about his friend in Philadelphia, a composer whose "Orphans of the Opera" originally inhabited operas of Debussy and Berg. He'll bring them to the class, no, not the entire operas, just a few moments of the scenes...and someone asks if he will play the flute for them. If they are good, he promises—if they double space and take pity on that imaginary reader whose mantle he must wear for them this semester, he will play for them at term's end, a piece Harold wrote for him. The magical and beautiful piece he once promised James. It was a birthday present twenty-five years ago. His graduate students prattle on swimmingly and James muses, having only to be reminded when the class time has expired.

*

Even after several weeks of teaching, James still becomes confused by the sameness of the long darkened hallways of the library building. After a particularly engrossing undergraduate workshop he discovers he is lost again—nothing seems familiar. Finally, he finds himself looking into an open office. There is a lamp, some kind of antique with colored glass in the shade, which glows a soft orange and, instead of a desk, a table with a fringed cloth. A white-bearded man is sitting in a padded chair with a book in his lap, looking as if he were waiting for someone. James has already paused in the doorway too long not to explain himself.

"I know you," the man exclaims suddenly, pulling himself up from the chair with considerable effort. He appears to be in his seventies and puffs with the effort of rising from the chair. James thinks his untrimmed beard is impressive.

"You're my new colleague—I didn't attend your reading—I was unwell—but I got all the reports—it's James, isn't it?"

"James Baxter."

"Yes, of course—Elliott Weisman—Poetry. Emeritus. You know—but I still teach—students come to my house—I come here as well—now—sit down with me. I'm an old man. I need to sit."

The man puffs for a moment, then drops into the easy chair.

"Now—We'll talk. You've been upstairs with the undergraduates? They sit around like frogs and wait for you to bring them a dragonfly? And if you move too quickly, they startle and jump? "

James smiles. They had been frustrating, unwilling to criticize the manuscripts they read. He suspects it will take him the better part of the semester to piece out their relationships, ranging from new romances to old grudges.

"Make them move the furniture."

James looks at Elliott. He holds his hands on his prominent stomach, fingertips touching.

"Yes, of course, make them move the furniture. If the chairs are in rows, move them into a circle. My classes always move furniture. We work, cooperate. Tables scrape. They misplace their backpacks. End of class, do the same. Out of the body into the mind. Out of the mind, into the body. Then after time, we read a poem. Here, I put it on the table. Then you. You come to the poem."

James rises from his chair and walks to the table where Elliot has put a sheet of cream-colored paper. As James looks at the carefully copied poem, Elliot recites the second half of the poem, his robust voice suddenly quiet:

These are brand new birds of twelvemonths' growing,
Which a year ago, or less than twain,
No finches were, nor nightingales,
     Nor thrushes,
But only particles of grain,
    And earth, and air, and rain.

"It is Hardy, of course, but they have come to him in this way. It would work with Colley Cibber. It works with their own poems. They lay them out on the tables they have moved together. They walk around, as if they were viewing paintings. They are extracted from their own world and enter the world of the poem. Of course, with fiction, you'll need a very large table—a large table, indeed."

Elliot's voice is resonant again and James listens more to its sound than its meaning. He will have to do something to enliven his class. Perhaps bring Elliott to visit. They had all seemed relieved when James assigned them papers to write.

*

Andi is probably his best writer, a graduate student with an independent study project who comes to his office dressed variously in overalls, something that looks like a little girl's party dress, miniskirts—and even the black costume with stacked heels that all the Asian students wear. Her entrances distract him—it takes him more than a moment to recognize his student in her disguises, who keeps giving him stories about young girls seducing fifty-year-old men. They are well-written stories, and the sex is understated. Still, he feels as if he is reading instructions for a do-it-yourself project.

"Why are these girls always showing their underpants to old guys?" he asks her after only the second story. Andi has a thin face and her teeth are a little strange—rabbity almost. But she has great eyes, and a way of looking at him, that is, he realizes, very much like girls showing their underpants to old guys.

She has great eyes? What student would he let get away with that? It's what she does with her eyes. She doesn't blink. She looks at you too long. It's the sort of thing a child might do. Or a woman with purpose.

"I'm working on some other stories," she says, "but . . . " James gets another look.

He finds himself reflecting that he isn't as old as the characters in her stories and that she isn't as young.

"Girls get interested in their professors sometimes," James might begin, "because they give a good show. . . . "

"What I like about this professor," Andi gets up and shuts the door—"is just that there isn't a show. And I can wait until this semester's over." Perhaps the door is already shut—the hallway is noisy.

James will compare himself later to the older men in Andi's stories.

They are thoughtful, resist the advances of the young women with fatherly concern, usually succumbing only after some terrible loss or hardship. James will have taken Andi home with him that afternoon. It could happen later, but why bother with all those scenes?

*

He notices the bugles and trumpets planted in the lawn next door have been replaced with silverware—knives, forks, crank-handled eggbeaters. Even a colander he considers liberating—it seems new.

"Does this mean I'll get an A?"

"It probably means I'll get fired. If my housemate ever shows up, he's sure to recognize you."

"Would that be a plot element that would draw us into this narrative—this concern for your well-being, your livelihood? Will the little hussy turn you in and notch her gun?"

"Not much of a story, Andi. I've got a notch, too. I'm teaching a Zen poet to my undergraduates. His name was Ikkyu and he carried on with a young girl when he was 77. Of course, that was the 15th century and she was blind. I'll try to write you a few poems before you dump me."

"So our story is going to suck?"

It is the shape of her mouth, he decides. All along there was something there he was seeing—some connection. An old girlfriend? A cartoon character? He can't put his finger on what it is, but he was seeing it. Perhaps a scent, or an ultra-high frequency. That moth business. There are spiders that counterfeit pheromones of moths. Still, when he kisses her, he can taste it. It's not like bubble gum or sour metal or the shape of that odd overbite. Better not get overly clinical. Lips soft. Softer before they touch. All in the imagination.

"What's a job? Nobody cares about other peoples' jobs."

"It's no big deal then?"

"It's no big deal."

This is as much as they will say to each other. And they will say it after they have made love—and sometimes during. So it will become. No big deal.

*

He couldn't find Harold's number. It is the kind of coincidence that no one ever believes, that would never work in a story. He was going to call him and tell him about the Orphans of the Opera business—come to think of it, another impossible coincidence—and he had his Rolodex and the phone both in his lap. When the phone rang, he dropped them both. The call is from a woman named Alice who James remembers vaguely from the time he and Harold lived with the others in the communal house on Delancey Street.

Harold and James had been students together—they had met in the sixties, lived in that big house, joined an Islamic religious sect, danced dervish circles and spoken in tongues—Harold had followed the guru to Indonesia and back—James had remained in Philadelphia, and then migrated south, an outsider to the end, managing always to achieve more headaches than enlightenment. Over the years, however, they had kept in touch, exchanging stories, poems, and plays; planning, and sometimes actually performing (but that was years ago), Harold's compositions. Harold has been living alone in Philadelphia for the past five years—now he works in a little vitamin store on Sansom Street. When he first moved into that apartment, Alice had been his roommate—it hadn't lasted long.

James holds the phone against his other ear. It is hot and his head hurts and Alice keeps going on about the drugs Harold has taken and the stomach pump and the charcoal they have fed him. He is safe in the hospital, but then Alice cannot decide—is he really safe?

After Alice hangs up, James calls the number she has given him and hears Harold's voice. It is all true, apparently. Harold's voice is all there is of Harold, and it is thick, like a syrupy dream.

"I feel like Sigourney Weaver in *Ghostbusters*. I'm six finches above the bed, hovering. No that's not it. Six . . . six inches. How much is that in meters?"

"What happened?" James asks him.

"I took all my pills. Too much talking. Voices bother me."

"Harold." Silence. But James can hear Harold breathing. He can't decide whether it is his voice or other voices Harold is mumbling about, and says something inane like be well before he hangs up.

There's a line early on in Pynchon's *The Crying of Lot 49* about a disconsolate melody from the fourth movement of the Bartok *Concerto for Orchestra*. James wonders whether it was the first statement of the melody old Tom had in mind or the retrograde—he is hearing both.

      The next day, Alex, orphaning his "Orphans," brings a story to the graduate workshop told from the point of view of an invisible monkey. The undergraduate workshop has recently discovered the joys of explicit sex and seems to be playing Can You Top This. There was a bathtub sex scene in the previous session in which two characters indulged in foreplay consisting of screaming "Do you want it?" Perhaps these are lunar trends, or something like weather fronts, James ponders. The character in the bathtub has a sunken chest, a depression from which he can eat cornflakes. James admires this detail, and does not insist, as a teacher of his once did, that it lacks value because it has obviously been mined from "real life."

      "Why must the monkey be invisible?" James asks, bringing about lengthy discussion, and a four-page letter from Alex will be waiting for him in his box tomorrow.

      Harold is released from the hospital, but the drugs he has been given to silence the voices give him a palsy. Also, his vision is blurred. He cannot work at the vitamin store.

      "You know I've been playing the solo piece."

      "My piece?"

      "Really, I think you ought to get it set with one of those computer programs and send it around to publishers. I found your original copy in my stuff. It's got my poem on it. You wouldn't mind leaving that out, would you?"

      "No way, I like that poem. It's about a toad, my favorite animal."

      "It's about a crow as far as I can tell. I see better work in my class."

      "No way. It's better than that bug piece you sent me, too. You've just lost touch with yourself. You're so old, it's getting like fighting with your father."

      "How are your eyes?

      "Remember that 50s sci-fi movie, the one where we get to see what the alien sees, and he's kind of an upside down garbage can with one big eye—and it's all watery and wavery? Well, that's what I get but without the theremin. I am Polyphemus. No man has stuck his finger in my eye. Dr. Israel No Man to you, my shrink. He's trying to tune the drugs.

"Well, hang in, Polly. He'll get it tuned."

"It won't be well tempered, the thirds are way too low."

Sometimes when James calls there is no answer, or worse, a thick voice which seems to belong to no intelligence whatever, one which struggles a few moments with words, or something larger than words, before the line clicks off. James feels then as if he has been caught in an expanse of sucking mud, that his boots have pulled off somewhere behind him and he is sinking amid a foul smell.

Harold has no recollection of these moments, posits wrong numbers. He is bright when he appears in his own guise, but tires easily.

"You know John Gardner was killed in a motorcycle accident. The Mormons got him. What did you do with your motorcycle?"

"I sold that motorcycle a long time ago."

"No you didn't. You're taking your pretty students for rides, aren't you—and keeping the thing in low gear. It's sly, predatory. I'm proud of you. But you've got to watch out for the Mormons. They've got gold buried in their yards, or maybe it's butter—anyway, they're certainly watching you."

"Harold, what are you doing with your meds?"

"I miss those little paper cups the nurses had. Tiny little cups. One for each Mormon."

"Harold."

"Good night, Gracie."

*

On Thursdays, James has lunch with Victoria Stone, a poet—Victoria came to his office the day after his reading to congratulate and welcome him. Lunch in the student cafeteria with Victoria is a rare grown-up time for James, despite the passing smirks of some of his graduate students. Once Victoria asks him if he thinks Andi is a promising writer. He studies her face for secrets but sees nothing. Does James know Elliott is planning on giving a reading? It might, God forbid, be his farewell to the University—his health has been so bad these past years. James ventures that he thought Elliott the picture of health and Victoria begins an exquisitely focused presentation on Elliott's illnesses, his mysterious intestinal bleeding, the trips to the emergency room, subsequent anemia.

James watches the students passing in the lunchroom, occasionally acknowledging a familiar face, while Victoria continues, passionately reciting. How we love our bodies' failings, James thinks. In each of us, the plunging airplane, the locomotive bearing down upon a crosswalk, tornadoes, floods, flames, ticking bombs, creeping predators—threatened heart, lungs, kidneys, intestines—our dear bodies, our dear disasters. And Victoria chatters on, radiant, until their plates are clean and they take them to a window made of stainless steel.

And, how like Victoria, there is a note for him in his office, and not for the first time—she feels he should devise some kind of performance piece—somehow manage to have his flute in hand when he reads again. He is a writer. He played in that orchestra for all those years. Surely he can bring those two things together, if not for the entire University, at least for some of the students. James folds the note and sighs.

He read poems and improvised on bamboo flutes when he was scarcely older than these students stretched out on the floor in the corridor as they wait for their appointments with professors or TAs. James' office is in the basement, among the ones shared by graduate students, just on the wrong side of the tracks. Discouraged-looking English composition students file like ants in and out of the dim offices, brightening only when they meet their friends, lounging and contorted in the hallway. "Poems and flute improvisations." James remembers a little gallery, nearly empty—Harold had been there, and afterward had critiqued their structure, which he claimed to have discerned—he had made notes on the program—James had rigged a tape recorder to make a several-second delay so he could play echoes and duets with himself. What would he think now if he could hear that evening again? Only the impossible can remain wonderful.

It is when he tosses Victoria's letter in the trashcan that he notices his blinking message light.

Alice again. Repeat of scene. But worse this time. There is concern over possible brain damage. She is calling from Boston because her mother has had a stroke. She can't handle all this, gives James phone numbers. James calls Jack, another composer, one of the few friends from those old days who still live in Philadelphia. Jack lives in the neighborhood of the hospital where they're not releasing any information—he can go there and find out what is really going on.

But Jack turns out to be incoherently drunk. Another detail from real life, James thinks.

*

Andi brings him the first 100 pages of a novel. It contains two parties and a great deal of shopping. She, too, had apparently been inspired by the visiting writer. James has begun to think of that novel class in terms of a catastrophic event, like the Permian extinctions.

The setting here should not be James' office at the university, but his study in the tall house on Lincoln Ave. Gordon, a furtive figure hunched over in a trench coat, scurries out the front door and drives away in a rusted car. All this takes place slightly faster than is possible, the film searching for something. James and Andi. James' desk is a door on wooden filing cabinets. He tells her he likes her novella, noticing for the first time the odd mixture of dust bunnies, paperclips, and broken pencils under his desk. It seems to have become a single substance.

You hate it, Andi says. And why call it a novella? I only hate my own work, James tells her. And you can call it anything you like. You just wish it were shorter, she says. Is this character, the woman who goes to the parties after she tells everyone she isn't going to—is she going to hook up with the clever young man who knows the complete history of quilting? Does he mean "hook up" in the sense that the term is used on the campus, or does he imply some kind of less specific connection? Andi's voice has an edge James has not heard before. Subtext, he thinks, or perhaps he says. Does it matter what they are talking about? Why would a young girl (a young woman) want to have anything to do (to hook up) with him? The young man of quilting fame? No, the old writer. Does the word on the page escape its mortality? Of course. But the paper yellows. The manuscript becomes artifact, as does the man.

"Let's go for a walk by the river."

"We can't go out. They'll see us."

"I don't care if they see us."

Disembodied dialogue. Have they said the lines? And whose lines were they? Does James care if he is seen with Andi or does Andi care if she is seen with James? Or were these just voices like Harold's? James has emptied a liter and a half bottle of cheap white wine. There has been no walk by the river but they have made love.

Hooked up. No problem. The air is still thick with the complex smell of lovemaking. Complex like fish heads. This is setting.

*

The telephone. Elliott, ubiquitous, here also a neighbor. Merely a block away (an implausible coincidence, James would be the first to note) and certainly reason enough not to walk by the river with a student who writes stories about young girls standing on their desks in school and removing their underpants while the other children cheer. Elliott is writing James a letter of recommendation, has been hard at it for the past six weeks. Now he realizes, while he has read the slender volume of James' short fiction, he has not seen any of the poems. He wants to know if James will bring him a batch of them now. James begs him to wait until tomorrow, he will bring them to school—it's the day Elliot comes in to his office, anyway. But this ploy isn't working—Elliott is in the mood to read some of James' poems. Who wanted the recommendation, anyway? James is feeling feverish and knows Elliott doesn't drink. He's writing this very minute, that's it, he's finishing a poem. Okay, Elliott agrees, without guilt. James shouldn't have answered the phone—he wouldn't have. What's the first line, then? No problem, James says.

*

After Elliott, James feels as if he really has been working on a poem. He wanders through the empty house listening to the mournful creaking of the stairs. He finds a half full bottle of cognac that Gordon must have left and pours an inch into a measuring cup, the only clean container he can find. The cognac seems to clear his head. He has been reading John Gardner. *Mickelsson's Ghosts* is, he thinks, a very fine book. And out of print—not a good omen for the rest of us, James thinks. And stacked under it, more reading, *The Art of Fiction* and *On Becoming a Novelist*. James has told his classes repeatedly about Gardner's notion of the vivid and continuous fictional dream. He tells them the ghost of John Gardner is looking over their shoulders as they write. A gust of wind rattles the kitchen window and James notices that it has begun snowing. He gets Andi's machine and manages not to leave a message.

A week later, Elliott gives him a lovely letter of recommendation, describing the poems James has never shown him. James has had two more conversations with Harold, who is now resting at home, has been assigned a new psychiatrist, and is remarkably cheerful and optimistic. Like Elliott, he wants to see some of James' new poems— just type them in a big-assed font—Harold is listening to *Das Lied von der Erde*, an old Philadelphia Orchestra recording. Harold is always listening to the likes of *Das Lied*.

Andi has come by his office with a story about an old woman who loves to garden and talks to elves in the pumpkin patch. In this scene Andi says she needs a little space—a little time. Time and space, James says. Good choice for you, but do you mean like *Scientific American* time and space or 60s time and space? Apparently this is a rhetorical question. No problem. The light on his office telephone is blinking. No one ever calls him these days but Alice.

Her voice is flat and seems even more tired than usual. James can count on Alice to produce Joycean detail concerning Harold's health, no matter how little sleep it has given her. In this message, she only asks him to call her—James sits before his gray metal desk with his head in his hands. A high-pitched laugh comes from the hallway. He hasn't bothered to decorate his office beyond a poster for the Bread Loaf Writers' Conference and a clock that produces the guttural sounds of New World frogs on the hour. *Bufonidae, ranidae,* and *hylidae.* The last hour was Couch's spadefoot toad—an interesting little creature which spends most of the year buried in the earth— *pelobatidae.* In the spring rains, they come up in swarms to mate, their calls like loud snoring.

James enjoys the effect the clock has on his students who have come for conferences. The bullfrog caused one girl to rush out into the hall. While his window looks out principally upon a parking lot, there is a rise of ground beyond it and a procession of students bends before the wind, perhaps like something in Breughel—*The Triumph of Death* with its horizons of skeleton armies comes to mind. A UPS truck grinds away outside his window and he smells the diesel fumes instantly. Perhaps it is his imagination. Writers are always imagining things.

He will call Alice, but from home, the child's-drawing house on Lincoln Avenue next to the magic land of knives, forks, and planted eggbeaters where the crow is the ruling animal, calling from above and wickedly piercing the plastic garbage bags laid out in offering on the sidewalks. And she is waiting for him, it seems, there not being a large audience for this final narrative. She found Harold in his apartment after he failed to call over the weekend. He had been dead a day—two days. She says it was a massive heart attack but James wonders how the doctors could know such a thing. She had to wait in the apartment for the police to come. There was no note—his medicine was all in place. There had always been more than the voices, all kinds of physical failings. Does James know Harold had a child? Yes, he knows. Does she need help with the arrangements? No, Jack, finally sober, has come and made himself useful. There are a few scraps of family left. Everything has been done that is needed. Perhaps there will be a memorial service. Harold's ex-wife will decide. James thanks Alice for calling him; and after a few more clinical descriptions of the condition of the body, she is done.

James remembers the house on Delancey Street where he lived with Anna and Harold and the others. He can hear the piano from the empty dining room, late in the afternoon—Harold testing the notes of the flute piece he is writing for James—like hesitant birdcalls, persistent, questioning. James listened in the butler's pantry, thinking how strange his life had become, that he should be in that place listening to those odd wisps of music. Later Harold would present the piece to him as a gift, calling it "Music for a Poem." The poem was one James had given Harold, featuring, he recalls ironically, crows. He had lost his own drafts and considered it safely forgotten, although Harold had copied it in his fine hand on one of the scores. Then the score had turned up in his music cabinet, like a corpse thrust up by frost, misfiled all those years.

The wind picks up and is moving the branches of the bare maple tree against the attic window of James' study. The phone reminds him he need not be alone. He could call Andi. Perhaps after a week . . . Too late to introduce another character . . . especially the brunette with the big boobs from the graduate workshop, although Harold would have approved. He looks in the small briefcase of music he has brought with him. C. P. E. Bach. Taffanel-Gaubert exercises. Prokofiev. There it is, new and spiral bound, in the oddly impersonal computerized notation he had been planning to surprise Harold with.

"Elliott, have you got half an hour? I want to play something for you."

James walks two blocks in the wrong direction before he notices. Somehow, Elliott must always be approached indirectly, the traveler lost, then found. It is still light, but he has no idea if he is disturbing Elliott's dinnertime.

The old man is cordial, but he doesn't offer James anything. He puts his fingers together the way he probably does for his students and sits on the edge of a chair.

"This is something a friend wrote for me a long time ago. I had it typeset, but I have his original manuscript somewhere at home. The manuscript paper's gotten yellow and it's starting to fall apart. He died—my friend, a few days ago, and I'm going to play this piece for his memorial service. I'd like to play it for you because I don't know what it will be like for me—I've performed all my life, but this won't be a performance—I mean it doesn't matter if I play all the notes correctly—it's something else—I'm not sure what it is. That's why I'd like to play it for you. Perhaps I'll learn."

Elliott nods his head slowly and, placing his hands on his knees, assumes an even more patient and expectant posture.

James realizes he hasn't played in weeks. He sets the music stand in the center of Elliott's small living room and assembles his flute. This is what it was like for him to play for his parents or for company when he was a young student.

It is not a long piece—a slow melody with a flurry in the middle, the slow melody returning after the activity. James thinks as he is playing that it is rather like passing a landscape as one walks or perhaps rides slowly in a carriage. Here is the measure that Harold had asked him to play more quickly. They had spent the better part of an afternoon on this measure—quick short notes which interrupt the slow melody—he could not seem to find what Harold wanted. Now the measure has fallen behind. A truck passes in the street. James wants to slow the piece down, to draw it out, make it stop, even; but it plays on despite his thoughts. It is a sad melody, he thinks, even though he can remember part of a line of the poem, "out of the rain joyfully." Out of the rain. Out of the rain. What in the world does that mean? The last note has a fermata— it should last and diminish and become for a while both present and absent, present and past. James plays the note until it ends. He will have to practice to be able to hold the note and diminish it cleanly.

"It's a fine piece," Elliott says, breaking the silence, and his voice, too, breaking slightly. He seems moved.

"Can you imagine that he was thinking about something joyful?" James asks.

Elliott puts his fingertips back together and bobs his head. James can't decide whether he is concurring or merely thinking. That habit of the academic. Visible thinking.

James returns his instrument to its case and looks around the darkened room. He will dream this night that it is stolen or lost. Elliott still seems content to remain in his chair, to remain still, to become shadowy. "Rain the green the rain the crow-green rain." Another line. Why in the world had Harold chosen that awful poem? But remember, music is only about itself, like numbers.

James thanks Elliott and it is only as he is passing out the door that the older man becomes his voluble self again, inviting him to stay, to have tea, to discuss music, to plan a joint teaching project. But James is able to slip away when Elliott succumbs to an old habit—excusing himself suddenly to rush into the other room and jot down a few lines which have just occurred to him.

The memorial service has been postponed, but James plays once again for his students on the last day of classes. Victoria has insisted that he develop a reading/performance piece and James realizes she has good instincts—to writers, he is more interesting as a musician. To musicians, he muses... when would you ever catch a musician at a poetry reading? So he has written a kind of prosy poem about what it is like to perform—and he will play Harold's piece in the course of the reading. It is to be linear—one thing and then the other, nothing simultaneous or accompanied. That would be too much a performance. Somehow, he thinks, he is trying to take the performance out of performance.

James has invited both Elliott and Victoria, but Elliott is still recovering from a recent hospitalization. Even his independent study students are present, all of whom, including Andi, he has given A's. The students are excited—everyone is going to read their work for a final time; but to begin things, James has agreed to play and read. James looks for Harold's music in his briefcase and realizes suddenly that he has left it at home. He can see it on the music stand in his attic study. He had been packing—this is his last day—most of his things are already in his car—there was so much stuff, he had been forced to take the books out of their boxes and slide them in between pieces of furniture. Then he'd practiced. Always the mistake. The only times in his life he'd ever forgotten music had been because of last-minute practicing. And there isn't time to get it.

So he reads his poem and in it a small tribute to his friend Harold, then pretending to read from the poem, goes on: The night's outside again, but we're in this room with our little light, our memories, whatever has touched us. The night's the same always, walking around the world. Look here, to this light, my friends. Wash in it, call it names, see in it colors, green, crow, feel it in rain. Now outside, the world is spilling dark, the oldest, that crow-dark shadow, outside the windows, it's falling. Or perhaps even, we're rising in it. James takes his flute, and after pausing for a long moment, he raises his flute, seems to listen, then his arms drop. Finally, he raises the flute with purpose and plays the solo from the end of Mendelssohn's scherzo, a flurry of sixteenth notes, all he can think of—Harold's piece, all the Mozart, the Bach, have washed away. The only music he can find is this, cheerful, half fantastic. And when he finishes, the students cheer. Victoria kisses his cheek.

A final scene: It could be the night James leaves Elliot's house— it could be this night, his last in Binghamton. They will be linked for him in his memory always. He has been walking on Beethoven Street and realizes he has chosen the wrong direction. No, it's not a dream. No one can get lost like this twice in the same place, he thinks. Unless this place has become a maze, reversing itself. What a useless thought. Chill damp air has worked its way up from the river—standing at a cross street he thinks he can smell the river, its muddy banks, trees and snags wedged like broken pencils and the water passing darkly beneath, giving up its scent.

> Hey diddle diddle, the cat and the fiddle,
> the cow jumped over the moon—
> the children laughed to see such fun,
> and the plate ran away with the spoon. . . .

The spoon. Where are the spoons? James is standing at the corner house and the garden silverware is missing. But then he sees what he imagines at first are merely round stones. Bowling balls. Perhaps a hundred. Arranged in careful rows around the flowerbeds, the ivy. A few gleaming with drops of the icy rain that has begun to fall. James climbs the steps to his porch slowly and turns toward the street before going inside. Lights shine behind windows. Everyone is warm and safe. Down in the next block, Elliott is writing a poem—perhaps the nights are long for him.

Across the river valley, which James imagines he can see behind the row of houses facing him, there are lights, perhaps even from the library tower on the campus—a place where students are studying, safe also for a time. Here he is guarded by this whimsy. Bowling balls which on a cross street might roll all the way to the river. Perhaps they have been anchored. Voices. That disconsolate melody with its repeated notes that follows him like a stray dog, and the soft clatter of bones falling in the street, a seething like icy snow in tree branches. James turns, unlocks the door, and climbs to his attic study. The voices are indistinct, but the closing door has no effect on them. One says "the plate ran away with the spoon." Another, "rain the green the rain." He is not thinking them. They are voices, voices with timbre, character, a bit high-pitched, perhaps. Occasionally one breaks into soft laughter.

Two Short Pieces
Philadelphia, Nashville, 1985

Nashville
April 1985

Dear Harold,
Here's a piece I thought you might appreciate. Perhaps I should contemplate a sequence, moving next to *En Saga* (revenge on the clarinet), but then the clarinet is in itself sufficient revenge. Thanks for sending me the Kundera. I could never have conceived this waterfowl without it.

J

Swan of Tuonela

The *Swan of Tuonela* is a lovely mood piece and one of Sibelius' most popular works. Scored for solo English horn and strings and a few miscellaneous other instruments, it calms the mind and radiates that strange quality that inhabits all of Sibelius' music, a kind of brooding vision of wood and water, stone and sky. Since it is not scored for my instrument, the flute (surely in that case it would have been called the *Chicken of Tuonela*), I found myself resting in the front row of orchestra seats with a copy of Milan Kundera's *The Art of the Novel* during the part of the rehearsal set aside for Sibelius. I recall reading the chapter entitled "Dialogue on the Art of Composition" in which Mr. Kundera states that "There is nothing so dubious in a novel now—so ridiculous, so passé, so much in bad taste—as plot."

So, I thought, no longer are we bound by Chekhov's onerous rule that a gun observed in the first act must be fired in the last. I was deliriously imagining my success as a writer under those hospitable conditions when I was awakened from my reverie by the conductor bellowing at the orchestra, "No, no, play it big and round. Play it like

Brahms. Sibelius studied in Berlin, not Chattanooga!" I had always imagined he lived all his life in Helsinki in one of those moss-covered huts made of thousand-year-old telephone poles; but then, the history of Sibelius has always given me trouble. I love all his music except *Finlandia*; however, I noticed early in life that his portraits are identical to those of Paul Hindemith and Dwight David Eisenhower. Could they have been one person? Is this deconstruction? Then the loving swirling depths of the "Swan" swallowed me up again, and as I slipped into a deep dream, I wondered if the English horn could possibly be played in tune.

I was on a train, riding smoothly. I imagined at the time it was the Orient Express, but it looked a good deal like the Paoli local. Seated opposite me was a man I knew to be Theobald Boehm, the inventor of the modern flute, and I knew he was smoking Brahms' cigar. He was speaking to me in Serbo-Croatian, which is fortunate, because the only German I know is "Keck, launig, reichlich bewegt" which is written at the top of the *Caprice #20 f*or solo flute of Sigfrid Karg-Elert, which I think means "stick your G sharp finger in your ear; you won't need it in this piece, Buster." Boehm went on to confess to me that in the famous Boehm-Gordon controversy, it was he, Theobald, who had stolen Captain Gordon's patented flute design, and that the judgment of history was tragically incorrect.

"It all began," he said, "when I heard that limey Nicholson play his flute. I considered myself to be the leading virtuoso on the continent, but that guy could play so loud, he blew scenery over. Later I learned he had enlarged the holes of his flute with a cavalry sword, but by that time I had developed my schema for the design of a modern flute. I entered it in the Paris Exposition of 1867, but it was not awarded a prize because the judges took it for a design for a pay toilet franchise. Then I met Captain Gordon. He was a strange man. It was clear to me that he would end his life throwing his flute into Lake Geneva, you know, much the same way Joan Crawford walks into the ocean at the end of *Humoresque*. I stole his design, and now I must suffer for eternity, eating stale peanuts and smoking Brahms' cigar."

Someone shook my shoulder gently. "Time for the symphony." (We were also rehearsing a Beethoven symphony that day.) I blinked and made my way up to the stage. Why had I dreamed of Boehm? That Berlin remark, I suppose. I remembered a student of mine, a lovely girl whom I always associate with Boehm's etudes for flute. She used to wear a wonderful jump suit with a zipper all the way down the front. Ah, those were the days! Abandoned passion on my desk among the Karg-Elert *Caprices*. What a bounder I was. But all my students loved me. And I never gave a grade higher than B minus!

"Wake up! Time for the symphony!" I rushed to the stage and was able to assemble my instrument before the A was given. As we began rehearsing the symphony, it became clear the English horn player (who had been excused for the rest of the rehearsal due to his status as soloist) had chosen to practice in a room too near the rehearsal stage. His out-of-tune warblings caused the conductor to roll his eyes. Having fourteen measures rest, I quickly moved to the wings, and spoke to the stage manager. "Tell him we can hear him on stage," I whispered importantly. Then taking my trusty Kundera, I watched the manager walk into the practice room, and timing my action with the sudden cessation of the English horn, I slammed the book against the wall with a sharp report, took a deep breath, then walked back on stage. The orchestra had stopped and every face looked at me. "Right between the eyes," I said.

*

May 1985
Fishtown

Dear James,
I thought *Swan* was charming, but a little hard on Theobald B, our founder. In return, I offer this trifle. I have taken your weasel and Remener poems and set them in this fancy. Perhaps I did get a little out of hand. I showed it to Sid and he said he was baffled. I thought that was my line. Mike has family duty this weekend so I'm on my own. Taking into account your sensitivity on the subject, I have served up a straight persona for the weasel-poet, das Wieseldichter. There is something in each weasel, of course, which doesn't survive translation. Perhaps after my nap I'll send this by special messenger to the NY'r. Cheers,
H

Weasels

My obsession with weasels might have begun in the first days I lived in Philadelphia. I remember wandering in the vicinity of City Hall—I have always walked the streets at the noon hour, anxious to swim in the river of humanity, to sample bits and fragments of conversation blown by me like foam, to navigate, feeling the current, the spinning hidden snags, sand bars and mud shelves—I was in an eddy by Woolworths, with the words "O thin men of Haddam" numbly repeating themselves in my head, when I noticed her. An old woman with a ferret on a leash. The old woman and her leashed weasel moved slowly along the wall near the entrance to the store: she, bent over at the waist, the weasel, constantly lifting up its long body and weaving as it sniffed or watched—I could not decide— then down on all fours and up again, a hideous, comical twisting and weaving. I was forced to stare. The woman seemed to take no notice, held herself up with a short cane while the creature twisted, examining the displays, the wall, the air. Down for a few feet, then up to twine and dance. I could smell cigar smoke, bus exhaust, the scorched exhalations of hot concrete.

I hurried home and wrote my first weasel stories. In one, small children sang like robins from inside bamboo cages. In another, an old woman crossed a frozen river, only to die sleeping in the snow, her brown coat gleaming oddly as the snow melted in a slowly expanding circle, at the last obliterating the weasel tracks, which from above . . . here I broke off, having imagined only the corner of some large weasel revelation—something I felt the strength to lift and hurl at humanity, but my fingers, my hands, could not find a purchase. It was large, it was close, it was a shadow, then it was gone.

My Dear Sir,
I am sending you this weasel.
It was more than twenty years ago I began
my work—twenty years—but what is time to a weasel?
I know you have followed it with some interest.

My great poem was in several volumes,
and many who read it were converted.
A light shone from their eyes,
and they walked away with long,
determined strides.
Last week I was overrun by weasels,
and I'm sorry to report
they have eaten my manuscript.
I must, I know, accept this as an act of God.
It's not the usual thing.

They kept running under the legs of my chair,
catching my shoelaces in their tiny teeth.
Finally I was able to stun this one
with a translation of Baudelaire.
His breath smelled of glue when I caught him.

His little gut I think
contains my volumes III and IV.
I hope you will accept him as the fruit
of my long years' labor.
Watch out, he bites.

After I read the preceding poem to her, my girlfriend Emily began to insist we go on vacation. I had been working too hard. I had not been working hard enough. Her arguments were ambiguous but persistent. Eventually I agreed.

Driving through Vermont, we noticed a lovely field ascending to a copse of pine trees. The grass was green and tatters of a fine mist grazed above it.

"Let's stop, let's stop," Emily shrieked, excited as a child. We wandered in the grass, wetting our shoes. The air smelled of smooth round stones and the underbellies of clouds. The little wood seemed inviting although marginally dark and deep. At first I could not place the sound—an odd image of men wearing goggles and flowing scarves flickered in my mind—but then I noticed an enormous cloud of mosquitoes and Emily at its center.

"Run," I shouted, "Weasels are behind this!" Emily screamed. The little bloodsuckers had found me out, too. We streaked across the meadow toward the car, trailing black smoke. Some of those creatures were big as mayflies. In the car I turned on the radio for some music. Emily turned it off. "Nasty bugs," I said. "Watch the road," Emily replied without moving her lips.

The next day we arrived in Maine and "our great Atlantic Ocean" as our landlady put it. We gathered mussels, snails, and quahogs. The clams we cooked and ate, and soon suffered the torments of the damned. We were almost recovered when it was time to return to Philadelphia. In my delirium, I had dreamed and spoken of weasels. A six-foot weasel had come through the bedroom wall but, halfway through, perhaps because it had materialized too quickly, it became firmly wedged. "This is another fine mess you've gotten me into," it said.

Emily was pleased to have lost the five to ten pounds but, as soon as we unpacked, announced she was going to visit her sister in Tucson.

In her absence, I began a children's story, replete with rhymes. Its characters were a pair of fox-like creatures, the only animals I could draw besides weasels, and, of course, weasels themselves. I brought my main character, the lovely Remener, toward the dangerous evening hour. I felt that my plot was shaping itself toward a mighty climax.

Here I quote from my fragmentary work:

But on her way home
she must pass through the weasely wood,
the darkest, the meanest,
the coldest, the deepest . . .

. . . strange sounds, wild hoots,
oozed from the tangle,
uncomfortably like
weasels with warts on their noses
and moths in their clotheses.

The trees began bending
and drooping,
and the air became heavy
as if fat frogs were farting

and elephants pooping,
and spiders and grozels
and frap-dorps and fooples
were zorking and flerking
and snooking and ooping . . .

At this point I was disturbed by a knock at the door, my neighbor Jane, returning the bottle of wine she had borrowed a fortnight before. One thing led to another, as they often did in those days, and the next thing I can recall, it was morning. I had a fouler hangover than usual, and the taste in my mouth was something between old socks and new tennis balls. I also had several bruises, perhaps incurred by the sharp pelvic bones of Jane, a lively but slender girl. Now that I am older and wiser and, I should think, an infinitely more resourceful lover, it continually perplexes me that the world seems bereft of such friendly girls. Alas, Jane. But I digress.

I sat down to my frap-dorps with a strong cup of black coffee and discovered that my stately pleasure dome had foundered, slipped, and sunk in a mudslide, no doubt caused by flooding of the sacred river Alph. I could not recapture my muse.

Weasels, minks, martins, ferrets, polecats, stoats, ermine, badgers, wolverines, skunks. These creatures are slender, ranging in length from six inches to two feet. Their shape seems to have evolved through the necessity of pursuing rodents through narrow burrows. They (*Mustelidae*) share a gland, which can produce a strong musk or must, the efficacy of which is most renowned in skunks.

My weasels, as a rule, ranged midway in the spectrum between frap-dorps and badgers. They were distant creatures, a silhouette by the woodpile (precious few of those in Philadelphia), a rustle in the grass. That extended, interrogatory shape—the attitude of sudden listening, like an elementary particle sprung into being from its hiding place outside reality—was the weasel essence, das Wiesel Wesentliche.

I could not help wandering through the streets at noon, breathing the occasional thoughts of my fellow humans. Like the splat of a stray raindrop, one would burst open in my mind: "Clean the garage," "elephant carburetor," "musty debentures," "Nova lox, cream cheese, hold the onion," "Villains! dissemble no more! I admit the deed!" "change of underwear"—They passed me hurriedly, their auras streaming behind them like the smoke of so many choo-choos.

Their currents caused me to pass into an alley I had not seen before, and from this alley, I noticed, at right angles, another passageway. My eyes were still sun-dazzled, but I could make out on a distant wall some faint lettering: *Magic Theater, Entrance Not For Everybody*. When I squinted, the lettering disappeared, but there was a door with an odd ancient latch, and it stood slightly ajar. I heard strange scrabbling sounds from within.

Inside, the darkness was profound, but I was not deterred. I moved slowly until I stumbled into a chair. The gloom gradually dispelled and I could make out a woman, an old woman, seated facing me. She was the woman I had seen at Woolworths! I recognized the musky smell.

"We are pleased to have you for our midday meal," she said in a barely audible, crackly voice. I noticed that amid the packing cases and cardboard boxes (we seemed to be in a small warehouse) there were furtive movements. Little heads with close-set ears suddenly appeared and disappeared, bobbing up into the faint light, and jerking back down into the thick gloom like so many fishing floats sucked under by sharks or alligators.

For a moment I was filled with sadness, but then I remembered my harmonica. I had left it on a bookshelf when I was a child. I am sure my mother stole it. Imagine the conclusion of this scene: weasels dancing to an uncanny melody—where would it have led? But no. I had a piece of old chewing gum in my pocket. Some lint. My mind was wandering. The little creatures were sniffing about my legs now. I sat motionless, trying to calm my breathing. I thought to try to whistle. A show of insouciance might be appropriate. A Bruckner symphony, Webern's *Opus 9*? My mind was muddled, I simply could not decide. Then I felt them pulling at my shoelaces.

A WOMAN'S NAME, IN THE DARK
Nashville, 1978

I remember that first rehearsal, but it's an odd memory. I can see the stage, the hardwood boards—I must have climbed up from the orchestra level, vaulted over the footlights, found my chair in the jumble of woodwinds, castoff clarinet reeds already littering the floor—and that floor—it was old and the finish had been scraped off by feet and chairs and risers. It was dusty and gray and the bright afternoon light which came in through enormous venetian blinds hanging from the tall ranked windows washed itself in dust. Dust settled and dust rose, and the light above the old boards enjoyed the muddle. Then I looked up and there was the hall, painted a color for battleships and park tanks, already peeling, the misaligned rows of seats and their stained cushions. It was noisy already and I unpacked my instrument and played a few notes. It's like the thing a carpenter does when he measures a room with his eyes. You play something, half a melody . . . and it comes back to you in the shape of the hall. No color, no dust, no sunlight. Just the hall, like a woman in your arms in the dark.

So it was a nice hall. Ugly, but live. It made me want to play again. Does it like Mozart? How hard do I have to blow? What happens when I play softly? This I couldn't tell in that moment because the brass had begun and the place was like a jungle at dawn. Probably it was too live, it was going to be difficult for the oboe and horn to hear the concertmaster when they play that melody together at the end of the second movement of Brahms' First Symphony. We discovered that to be true in the next concert, my first. And more was true—there were a lot of things you couldn't hear on that stage, but you could always hear the flute. I could tell that after playing five notes. I always can.

I had come to this orchestra from a season of playing chamber music, mostly small oddly configured groups. It had been interesting— but I wanted to play Beethoven and Brahms. And I hoped this orchestra would be a good one. I got my first wish, anyway. I loved the *Pastoral Symphony*. I love to play it, to feel it flowing around me, to hear my instrument above. I can look down and watch the world from that piece.

So it was in the Sixth Symphony, not the first concert, but nearly, and after the second movement, the "Szene am bach," the one that ends with the cadenza for flute, oboe, and clarinet, when the flute's slow trill is supposed to be a nightingale, and the oboe and clarinet are quail and cuckoo—it was then that I noticed her. She was sitting outside second stand of violas—well, I had noticed her before, but this time I recognized her. She had come to the door of my apartment looking for the woman who had lived there before me. I was looking for that woman, too. To try to find out if she had really intended to move out. I needed a place to live.

Where are we now—two women with no names—Kathy. That was my missing roommate. It turned out she had gone to Mexico to play in one of those orchestras that people can never stand to stay in more than a year. Kathy played the bassoon. I met her some time later. But the violist, Rachel, came to the door asking after Kathy. I had only been in town a few weeks and found this place after a friend told me it appeared to be empty. Rachel stood in the doorway, a tall girl with short black hair. I don't know what registered on me at the time, because I told her I didn't know where Kathy was, and she smiled and left. Nice smile? Something stuck with me and I kept getting that feeling when I saw her in the orchestra—that I knew her. Then, during the Beethoven symphony, I realized that I had seen her before in my doorway and that I loved her.

Nothing much to do then but to ask her out—for a drink or a ride on my motorcycle. In those days I did not have a very easy way with women, but I had learned to rely upon my own shyness. I had learned that it might often seem charming, and this gave me a kind of false courage. Still, courage is courage, and all that was needed was that I ask this young woman if she would like to . . . She politely declined before I had got to the motorcycle. "Really?" I said, stupid. "I have a relationship," she said and smiled again—something, I was certain, she only did for me. Her hair was brown, I saw then, and I liked her nose. Her lips were full, very white skin. Her neck, lovely, I thought, thinking also I must look like a fool to her. What does a fool look like? This one tall, bent over from the habit of looking down at faces, still wondering what to do about a very old homemade haircut. Mustache that might make sense in Montana but not here. . . .

She was gone and I found a place under one of those ranked windows and smoked my pipe for a while. It's almost painful for me to see this pipe smoking. It's the thing a dog who has been kicked would do if he could smoke a pipe. Still, it was soothing. I sat in the window on a seat that was some kind of entrance for the heating system into the hall. Warm air came up through a heavy pattern of holes in the metal. It had been painted a neutral color, so faded, and deposited so long ago, I could not identify it. The pipe smoke rose on the warm air, and my thoughts were tangled pick-up sticks. Stupid, stupid, stupid. They said also: Lovely, lovely.

I asked the oboe player, whose name was Robby, a happily married man with two young children, about her.

"Rachel, Rachel. Now if you're looking in the viola section, what about Chris? She has what Rachel doesn't. She has what few girls have. If I were you, I would ask Chris out. Oh my, oh my." Robby was a tit man. And Chris was the violist for his all-star team.

"And she's clean."

"What?"

"She's clean. That's important. You can tell she takes care of herself. Nice nails. Paints her toenails, too. Bet they take a long time to dry in all that shade." Much laughter—yes, mine, too. But Robby didn't know anything about Rachel.

So I asked Chris. It took me several days. And I could never have approached her. But I learned that I could sit on that window seat during the breaks and hold a book. People come up, "What are you reading?" They can't help it. It's like some kind of bait. For musicians, anyway. All right, what was it? *Journey to the East. Magister Ludi.* It was that time of life for me.

"It's about teaching," I told Chris, "how it's a noble thing."

"Nuts," said Chris cheerfully. And here the ghost of Robby shakes me by the shoulders for what I ask this woman with magnificent breasts who has come to me, the mountain to Mohammed, bringing them both along with her—now Robby is slapping me with his left hand, now the right. Yes, yes, I asked her about Rachel, I would tell him. She didn't seem particularly disappointed. She was just curious about what I was reading.

(Is Robby a ghost? No. Robby has merely dropped out of my life, and I do not expect to see him again. If I did, I think the conversation would begin to wane after the first sentence. He played very loud, and always when he began to play, before the sound of the oboe began, there was a sound that came from deep inside Robby, a suffering, choking, grinding, throaty noise. It didn't carry to the hall, but I could hear it. It was emblematic of his lifetime of struggle with the perverse instrument he played. Blow on your thumb, he told me once. Now blow harder and keep blowing until it comes out your ass. That's what it's like to play the oboe.) Chris told me she thought Rachel's friend was a lawyer. But that things might not be going too well.

Still, I was discouraged. Someone called me for a flute lesson. A woman. She showed up on a Saturday afternoon and there was a lot of talk, not much playing—something that often can't be avoided in first lessons with adults. She had grown up in this city, gone away to school, studied with a famous teacher in Chicago. She was going to audition for the opening in my orchestra. Our second flutist had announced her resignation after only a few weeks of being sniped at by me. I could look at her and she would say, "I know, I'm playing too loud and I'm sharp." Robby had tried to get me interested in her.

"Good lord, man, she's married," I said. "And besides, I don't like her." Robby kept going on about how clean she was. He had a hygienic fixation.

This auditioning woman, her name was Liz, was very ambitious, probably found out about the resignation before I did. She began to argue with me about a note in the Mozart Flute Concerto in G. I told her I thought it should be C sharp. She said the famous teacher in Chicago said it was C natural. She was very petite and strong-willed. She left me her phone number and said she would like to have lunch with me.

The next day, just as if aliens had left a transmitter implanted in my brain, I called her. She had a very perfect little body with tiny perfectly shaped breasts and a tiny waist. I was afraid I might break her so I let her get on top of me. It was like trying to hold a mad cat. I don't remember how I got rid of her, but I thought to myself, I'll hear that C natural in the audition, even if it comes from behind a screen.

Now, this is a story about love and stories about love will tend now and again to veer in the direction of sex. I could tell you about the hours I spent practicing because I spent them—they were necessary and important to my life. But they were just that. Hours spent. I'm not proud to tell the story of lunch with Liz. But it goes to establish the defendant's state of mind. I was a young man and the times were free—I was about to write "easy," but I can assure you that the times were not easy. If anything was easy, I would guess that I have forgotten it. Anyway, I did not have lunch with Liz again. I wonder now in this economy of time whether there are besides hours spent, hours earned?

The orchestra played along with its classical series a vast number (it seemed to me) of children's concerts. These were done in pairs—sometimes in triples. The children came into the hall in waves, bubbling and sparking like lava coming over the rim of a volcano. Then they subsided and were instructed and entertained—sometimes they responded to a repeated question from the conductor with a great shouted "good morning," loud enough to hurt our ears. Then they trailed out, hungry, loud, and fidgety, while more fresh prospects surged in to fill their places.

I performed over and over the first movement of a difficult flute concerto for these young music lovers. Well, they weren't music lovers yet—they were too young. What are you before you become a lover? I looked across the orchestra at Rachel with her viola tucked under her chin, an earnest expression on her face, and I knew what I was. "Horny," my friend Robby would have said. "In need of love," I would have corrected. I played the notes of my concerto from memory again and again. I could play them now if you were to hand me a flute. Isn't this an odd thing? All of these possibilities lurking in our minds like spiders, webs staked out, strung from one alien transmitter to the next. And in our hearts, the same thing. Not what Robby thinks. Not at all. But something waiting and languishing, ready to collapse into a mighty avalanche or to grow into a single, frail wildflower. After hidden years, like the locusts. It's all there, waiting.

Besides these concerts we also played pops concerts, but in another hall, larger and more expensive for the orchestra to rent. It was in another part of town, but there were walks and well-planted gardens around it. Inside, it was large and dead, nothing more than a sound stage, but we played there with wonderful musicians, Ella Fitzgerald, Benny Goodman. . . . I remember finding Benny Goodman alone in his dressing room, the door open, after his concert—I had never asked anyone for an autograph before, not even a baseball player, but there he was. I told him I admired his playing and that I had seen *The Benny Goodman Story* seven times. While he should have told me to get Steve Allen's autograph, he signed my program and told me he admired my pipe.

Once in the same hall, I mouthed the words "fuck you" to Arthur Fiedler during a performance—he reddened considerably, so it is unlikely there was any misunderstanding. And why? For the life of me I can't remember. He had been unreasonable during the rehearsal. When the moment in the music came, the unreasonable demand was made again . . . who knows, play louder, play softer. . . . I was an adolescent. In any event, it was a private moment between me and the maestro. The music, whatever it was, rolled on in spite of our mutual outrage.

The concert I am thinking of probably featured no famous artist. There was an afternoon rehearsal and a nighttime performance, the performance scheduled rather late so the symphony supporters could have a catered meal on the premises—it had something to do with fund raising. There was an open bar on the grounds for these affluent folk, and shortly after the rehearsal was over, I managed to slip in among the patrons and have several double Jack Daniels, Black Jacks, we called them. Then I wandered backstage and found most of the orchestra members still milling around, waiting for a lesser catered meal. And among them was Rachel. I was no longer shy. Come with me, I badgered. I'll buy you dinner. There are restaurants nearby. We can talk. And perhaps with as much a notion of keeping me away from the bar as anything, Rachel agreed.

We sat in a little Chinese restaurant and I told her that I remembered her from the first time I ever saw her, standing in the doorway of my shabby apartment, asking for Kathy, the girl who by now had returned from Mexico but didn't mind leaving me her place. I told Rachel that she was a vision that evening, that moonlight had glistened on her hair. I told her that I wanted to make love to her, that I was a wonderful lover, that I would make her very happy.

I know I said these things, I can almost hear myself saying them. I had never uttered such nonsense to a woman before, although I suppose most women have heard it often enough. After a while, I ran out of steam, and we ate our rice and vegetables quietly. It was rather nice, I remember thinking, as I began to sober up, to be sitting there with this quiet girl. And she was quiet. She had ignored my crowing and chest beating. It was as if I hadn't said a thing. After a while, it was time to go, and I asked her again in the car if she would see me another time. She didn't think so. But it was a quiet no. And we had talked some about subjects other than my prowess as a great lover.

The next day I was filled with remorse. But I reminded myself I would have been filled with remorse if I had not asked her to have dinner with me. And she *had* agreed to have dinner. The wheels of reckoning turned for me then as they do now. They never cease turning. Now, perhaps, there is more groaning and squeaking of the mechanism, but it is an unceasing business. Now I wonder about why a young woman would ever consent to endure such pestering. Perhaps I had a nice smile, too. Or when I sat in that window, she could see that I was lonely. Something about the mouth, unguarded, at its corners, like a secret language.

And did I give up—I was going to say "my dream" but this was no idealized Dulcinea. She was a real girl—rather quiet perhaps, which is a great aid to any imagination—pretty, but not beautiful, whatever that means. I gave up and I did not give up. I simply could think of nothing else to do. But she spoke to me across the forest of bows and music stands in the way that moths call each other in the night.

And then, a few weeks later, she spoke to me after a concert. It was her voice, not something I had manufactured in my own head in the final stages of lustful insanity, although I wondered for an instant. She said she would like to come home with me. Did I mind if she followed me in her car?

I had time to start the tape of *Pelleas et Melisande* which I was in the habit of listening to in those days. Dark, dark. Debussy opens with the very forest of my longing. And Rachel was at the door. I was kissing her before Golaud had taken his first breath. Now there is no dialogue in this scene. It does not become frenzied, either, at least for a time. I took her into the bedroom which was rather dark. She removed her dress which was a long black gown, the uniform for a symphony performance. I was wearing a tuxedo. Black tie for pops. White tie for Beethoven and Mozart. I remember regretting that there was this single garment for her to remove. I would rather, I suppose, have her a fabulous bird who must remove feather by feather. Melisande cried from the next room, "Ne me toucher pas," and ignoring this, I took Rachel into my bed.

I shall not stop here. It has been a long time and perhaps one night of love is like another. Or like the snowflakes I see now outside my window, always falling, or swirling around aimlessly. Perhaps it was the music.

I am not watching snowflakes, now. Rachel and I could not find a shape to settle into. We kissed. Our bodies touched. And in the way the wind disturbs the snow I am not watching now, our bodies rearranged themselves, as if they were not whole, discrete. I found myself kissing her in the most secret place and there was the odor of soil and roots—I nearly fainted. Then slowly as if it were ceremony, as it had surely become, I entered her, and for a moment we looked at each other, her brown eyes, mine not eyes to be seen—I cannot hover and watch these children—my eyes are invisible.

I felt the most terrible sadness of my life at that moment. Everything I had wished for had begun to end. I could see my life, past even these swirling snowflakes. I had become a wise man. Then I forgot—I was given the gift of that moment. Perhaps Rachel saw something, too. I wish I could know this. We began to move. In the next room Golaud's voice descended while the orchestra wove upward. In time, the tape came to an end.

In the early morning, she left. She told me she had a dog to take care of. I thanked her for a nice evening. I did. I could be gracious. It had seemed to me she had a nice evening, too. Then I did not see her again, as I suspected might be the case, for several weeks.

The next time she invited me to her house, and there *was* a dog, a small black dog. The place looked as if it had never been cleaned, but we found the bed. And there we made love which, on my part, was something as careful and as abandoned as any music I had ever made. And of real music, however, there was none, no *Pelleas* this time, just the sounds of the dog moving about. After a time, she fell asleep. I listened to her breathing and wondered if I could wake her to make love again. Instead I whispered as softly as I could into her ear that I loved her. It was the only time.

Once she called me in the middle of the day, cheerful, did I want to meet her for a quickie. Yes, the word exactly. The concertmaster had taken her to lunch and plied her with wine—he was a man in his fifties (as I am now), urbane (as I am not) and determined to bed this young girl. He was unsuccessful, but had put her in the mood, she told me. We had half an hour before her appointment somewhere. This experience was deeply disappointing for both of us and she agreed to spend that night with me, for a longy.

Now it would appear that I had achieved my heart's desire, and that, with a little patience, I could expect our relationship to deepen and—for those periods of weeks and more when she would only smile at me and shake her head—to diminish, shrink to nothing. But this did not happen. I would often become certain, in fact, that I had seen the last of her. As spring deepened, I would take my motorcycle for long rides in the evenings. It was a shaft-drive Yamaha that I kept in a garage down the street. Sometimes I took it to a large wooded park and followed the twisting roads slowly, breathing in a growing smell of earth and roots. Sometimes I rode fast, but I was not self-destructive. Later that summer I took it for a tour of several thousand miles. When I returned, just in time for an outdoor concert, I told my friends I was seeing the dotted white highway line in my music, that I would probably see it in my sleep.

As I was leaving the rehearsal, Rachel came up to me and said she would like to watch the dotted line with me. We had not been together for six weeks. So it was that our times together were like the first and never like what might have come after the first. My lovemaking had become ironically what I had advertised that night in the Chinese restaurant. I felt no need to sleep or to rest, only an immense unquenchable energy. A terrible quiet, like a great blanket, fell over us when we were together. We did not go for walks. Perhaps we cooked one meal together. We took off our clothes and pushed our bodies together. Then, most often, she would dress herself, and leave. Watching her put on her undergarments, I felt that first great sadness. This was such awful grief that once I stopped her, and impossibly aroused, made love to her again, against a chair, and then on the floor. I did not care if my heart would burst. I hoped it would.

Her father had treated her like a queen. She had a younger sister. There was another man. It was over. It was not. I would have to take things the way they were. This much the blanket allowed me.

Six months of this, I suppose. The intervening time has weathered out. I can't replace it. I could invent scenes, give us a lively relationship, but why? This is the story of a heart filling with despair, like a pond silting, becoming gradually shallower.

My friend Nancy said life is a shit sandwich. Your deal is you get to choose the bread. She and Hans had invited me to dinner. They did this often. Hans played the French horn. I had stayed at their house a week while I searched for a place to live. Nancy had lost a child in an ugly divorce. I told her my troubles. But I only came little by little to agree with her. I argued that I should take this girl as a gift. She came into my life occasionally. We were like the two sticks (I said this to Nancy) Boy Scouts rubbed together to make a fire. Then there was a warm fire. Then cold weeks. Nancy said, shit sandwich.

But in that disappearing pond: life, life. Frogs singing, hunting dragonflies, nesting birds and morning's music. Hans and I put together a recital of late 19th century salon music at the local college. The centerpiece was a romance for horn and flute, surely an unusual combination, a kind of paella of hunting horn calls and bird songs. Then, in an extended set of variations upon *The Carnival of Venice*, every instrument present played its most extravagant pyrotechnic passages, horn, bassoon, cello, flute. And violin. Larry, our assistant concertmaster, got a big time string quartet gig that spring. This was the last time we played together. For one of the variations we brought out a huge floor fan that had two speeds. As the accompaniment (which consisted of only two chords) changed harmony, the whirring fan changed speeds. This was Nancy's job. It was a great success with the audience and our best commentary on empty virtuosity. Rachel did not attend.

I hoped to play music with her and gave her the score and parts to the Debussy trio for flute, harp, and viola. She thanked me warmly, but nothing came of it. Perhaps the music was too difficult.

Is there no finale, then, to these variations? I can imagine, if I were inventing this story, any number of plausible endings. That motorcycle would do nicely. Or another job, another orchestra, particularly for Rachel, who I think played well. The viola is a useful instrument. Mozart and Beethoven both chose to play it on occasion. What did happen is this. During one of those insulating, empty periods between our bouts of fire-starting, I met another girl. We talked all night. We walked together. We prepared meals. Within a few weeks, I asked her to marry me. We were married in sixty days. I might have ridden that motorcycle into a bridge abutment. But that is another story. Nancy said, "James, you hardly know the woman." I shut my eyes and ears. Something was going to change in my life.

Another round of children's concerts—the week after our salon extravaganza. These feature *Peter and the Wolf*. Prokofiev's birdcalls are incessantly cheerful, more difficult than the flute concerto. I use one for my answering machine when I discover the beep is the same pitch as the last note of the call. The children bring great washes of cold air with them when they enter the hall. I retreat to my window seat nearest the stage and rub my hands over the rising warm air. Then I make my way to the stage, stepping over my colleagues, who do not seem to notice me. I have to change the message on my machine. Too many people are calling and hanging up, then calling again.

Now we play Hindemith: *Mathis der Maler*. The orchestration is inspired, leaving a single flute note to fill the hall after a tumultuous passage. I wonder at it. A single note. But the hall filled with it. We must all breathe it in, swim through it. It is a chilling, invisible thing. The drama is inescapable. The orchestra plunges on like a great whale diving in an abyss, then that single note again. I can imagine countless giant squid swimming beneath us, just out of sight, dim lights pulsating, growing brighter. Hindemith, however, does not go over well with the customers. They applaud politely. Some will write letters of complaint.

Sometime in that second month, before Gwyn and I were married, my phone rang. It was Rachel. She wanted to wish me well. I thanked her. There was a pause.

"I love you," she said.

"I know," I replied, not knowing in the least. My life might have changed again in that moment, but it did not. I hung up the phone.

One night in the week after I came back from my long motorcycle trip, this happened. Rachel had been with me every night for several days. I thought perhaps we had finally come together for good. We had made love so violently that night that we both cried out like animals, like cats, strange sounds which seemed more suffering than release. And I had fallen into a dead sleep. I woke suddenly with a sense of panic. She was gone. I could see this from the faint glow of the streetlight which filtered in the bedroom window. I thought I had heard the front door close. I wanted to call out her name, but I could not. I could not speak her name.

MARGARET
Nashville 1987, 1998, 2002

She said her name was Margaret. James had never had a student named Margaret, and when he asked her what her friends called her, she drew herself up at least an inch and speaking as formally as a ten-year-old with shiny new braces can speak, said again and with a strong accent on the first syllable, "Margareth."

James was teaching Tuesday afternoons at a community music school that had been named for a bass player he had known years before in the Symphony, an old-timer even then. The man had played with Duke Ellington, a distinction lost on the James of those years, but one which by now had begun to sink in. His name was B.B. Givings and he and the Duke were dead, but the music school had been funded and named after him. (He had been a cheerful, portly old gentleman whose left hand did not, James noticed, produce even a modicum of vibrato during symphony performances, and whose fund of off-color stories was not a part of his public legacy). In the B.B. Givings Community Music School, the teachers volunteered their time, and the students were poor—even the musical instruments were provided free of charge.

Margaret, however, had her own flute, a family treasure. While it was a long time before James consciously made the connection, Margaret had the same red hair, freckles and pale, almost transparent skin as his first high school sweetheart. He was smitten with her from the first day, and when she proved to have talent and perseverance, he was more than delighted. James showed her how to form an embouchure and blow a stream of air against her extended finger. She made a sound on the very first try, a rare occurrence for a beginner.

His first class of students at the B.B. Givings had not proven to be especially rewarding. Margaret was to fill the slot recently vacated by fourteen-year-old Amy, who had come to her lessons from a juvenile center, always escorted by a matron. After a protracted argument over whether the flute could be played by a person chewing gum (which became moot when Amy swallowed her gum), there was additional spirited discourse concerning the assignment, the music (provided by the B.B. Givings Fund) and other subjects peripheral, in James' opinion, to the matters at hand. Amy became loud and belligerent as opposed to merely belligerent and the matron burst in the door. James was fortunate enough to have been found sitting behind his desk and not in the compromising position of adjusting his grip on Amy's windpipe; in consequence, there was soon an opening in the B.B. Givings Tuesday flute lesson schedule. As Amy was escorted by the matron out the door of his studio, James did not fail to notice the miraculous reappearance of the allegedly swallowed chewing gum.

Margaret became James' star pupil that year, progressing from the *Rubank Method* to *40 Little Pieces for Beginning Flute Players*. Margaret especially enjoyed playing the minueths. Her tone became so robust that James invented an exercise for her to practice playing softly. Margaret called it the hush, be still game—she would play a piece from memory and when James suddenly held his finger before his lips, Margaret would drop the volume to a whisper. It was her favorite part of the lesson.

The next year, Margaret moved on to Händel and scales in all the keys and began to lose her lisp. Then, amidst the turmoil of an orchestra strike and lockout, the director of the B.B. Givings Community Music School, Edward Hatchet, a former Bostonian, no older than James, and whose fund of funny stories in all colors was deeper and broader than old B.B. himself, was killed in a bizarre automobile accident—one which he initially walked away from and only later succumbed to, one of his lungs punctured by a broken rib.

The school was closed for a time and then reopened under new management. While the students remained deserving, Margaret especially, James missed Edward's joke of the week, a man describing the taste of fried bald eagle as something between trumpeter swan and whooping crane, or the grotesquely altered anatomy of the man who had made the mistake of asking a magical mermaid for a little head. The new director was a woman whose first act was to move James to a cramped studio directly across the hall from the drum room. James gave notice. He offered to take Margaret as a private student and, as long as she was willing to practice, to continue giving her free lessons; but, for whatever reason, Margaret did not call at the end of the summer.

*

After a series of strikes and lockouts, the Symphony folded, to be reorganized only after much community effort and with a reduced schedule and lower wages for the musicians. Having written a book in his enforced spare time, James resigned, and became a college teacher of creative writing. Time passed. James wrote another book and read much student writing which called for improvement; though many of those students, James discovered, were not interested in improving their work. More time passed.

James spent a year teaching the novel in the Southwest. (On his first day he had been asked by a very wrinkled and possibly old woman in the mailroom if he knew why it was windy in Oklahoma— no, he said—because Texas blows and Kansas blows, she replied. Her merry cackle was interrupted by a fit of coughing, possibly induced by the blowing dust, a fine red grit.) In the spring of that dusty year, James received an email:

"Dear Mr. Baxter, do you remember me? It's Margaret! Guess what? I'm getting married! And I want you to play at my wedding. Please? Will you?"

Despite this incarnation as a visiting writer, James had never sold his home in the city surrounding the B.B. Givings School, and that was where Margaret planned to stage her nuptials. With only a faint sense of foreboding, much like the fine red dust pattering against his window, James agreed. The wedding would be in June. James made his way home toward the end of May, driving toward the rising sun, leaving behind him that odd state which seemed to contain only red dust, boat-tailed grackles, and mistletoe.

"Imagine," a colleague had lamented, "a place that makes a parasite its state plant, a place where rednecks stand on each other's backs in muddy rivers so they can stick their arms in the mouths of giant catfish."

"I can imagine," James said.

*

James had only been home a few days when Margaret appeared at his front door. She was not the chunky child James remembered, but a slender, strikingly attractive young woman. But when she smiled, James could connect her with the past more easily. There was a gap between her front teeth that she had learned to blow through in a kind of party trick, producing at the same time an almost acceptable flute sound and a Bugs Bunny face.

"I've brought the music I want you to play." James remembered that Margaret had always been businesslike. In a child it was charming.

"I want you to play the 'Meditation' from *Thais* and 'The Swan' and 'The Dance of the Blessed Spirits' and the Bach-Gounod 'Ave Maria' and something else by Bach but not 'Jesu Joy of Man's Desiring.' 'The Blessed Spirits' can bring in the mothers. The rest can go earlier in the prelude. There are three singers, a guitar player, and the pianist is Evangeline Marmaduke. She says she knows you. I have written a song for the bridal procession. Here. The music has Mrs. Marmaduke's instructions in it. Your rehearsal is next Saturday at 3:00—here's a map. We were going to have it at the school but it got too big. There are 200 guests so we're having it at the Unitarian Church."

James took the music.

"It's nice to see you, Margaret."

Margaret smiled the big smile James remembered.

"Who's the groom?"

Margaret had always had a tendency to talk fast and the subject of the groom seemed to send her into overdrive. Roddy was also a musician and had a very high grade point average and after the missionary thing didn't work out . . . of course, the two of them had been together since his father's car dealership caught fire. . . .

Waiting for Margaret to get to a breathing place, James found himself looking at the music she had handed him. It had been printed by a computer program and the higher notes requiring ledger lines were printed over with slurs and dynamic indications. He could see a few passages where it wasn't possible to read the pitches. But then, he knew these pieces.

"You know, Margaret, I haven't really been playing much this past year. Why don't you let me pick out a few pieces that are comfortable for me. You've got a regular flute recital here."

"Oh Mr. Baxter, Mrs. Marmaduke has picked out this music especially for me, and she said we might as well get our money's worth. Of course, you're playing for free, and that's really very generous of you. Mrs. Marmaduke is also the wedding coordinator and her husband is the photographer. Oh, I'm late. I've got to get the Balinesian chant to the guitarist. See you Saturday before the wedding."

Margaret dashed out the door, leaving behind swirls and eddies of low pressure: a bride with much to do, a young woman of conviction.

James set up a music stand and unpacked his flute. He played a few rusty, breathy notes. Nothing to worry about, really, if among the 200 guests no one had ever heard a flute played before. The "Meditation" from *Thaïs* was a solo written for the violin, an instrument which did not seem to involve as much gasping for air as James and his unfamiliar flute. "The Swan" was a solo written for the cello, likewise anaerobic. Ah, but the wedding was three weeks away. Like riding a bicycle, an old skill can be recaptured, the body can be bent to the purpose of the will. Vibrato can be rediscovered. A sense of pitch, of grace, would come, James told himself. One had only to endure the pain of listening—but wasn't this the way it had all begun, those many years ago? And didn't the sounds he was making remind James mostly of Margaret's Bugs Bunny trick?

"Is the flute a difficult instrument to play?" Musicians' jokes might seem a bit strange outside the orchestra. James remembered asking such a question earnestly of the clarinetist or oboist after any kind of mishap, careful attention paid to the straight face and the timing. Now he spoke for no audience save himself as he packed up the offending instrument, three sections of tubes constructed of sour metal, held to the side, out of sight if not out of hearing.

"Three weeks," James muttered to himself, just before the expletives resulting from his expensive silk flute swab getting caught in the zipper of the case cover.

*

Evangeline Marmaduke was a thin woman with worried, expressive hands. While she did not seem especially old, she carried herself with a pronounced stoop—she might have once been tall, but bending over keyboards had compressed her. There was something oddly familiar in her walk, but James couldn't place it. Her face was gray and worried, too—hair, eyes, nose, ears, all near their natural locations, but not quite, as if she were made of wax and the room was too warm. And the room was uncomfortably warm, and poorly lit—this was not an airy sanctuary, rather it seemed to have been decorated to resemble an Egyptian tomb, an odd design even for a Unitarian church, James thought.

"The 'Meditation' first? Two measures introduction." While there was the possible inflection of a question in Evangeline's voice, it was a rhetorical question.

"Mr. Baxter? You're not playing."

"I was making a note that there are two measures of introduction. There's no introduction in my music."

"Well, then. Surely you have played this piece before."

"Actually I haven't. I've avoided it for the past thirty years, but it seems to have caught up with me today."

"Miss Margaret told me it was her favorite of the selections."

"Then, by all means, let us play. Play is a curious word, don't you think? I've often found it to be nothing but work."

Evangeline raised an eyebrow, but said nothing. James had indulged himself with a wee toke on the way to his rehearsal. Perhaps he thought, as "Meditation" ground on to "Swan," it had not been in his best interest to so prepare himself—he seemed, now that he did not smoke regularly, to be more sensitive to the effects of weed. Time had slowed conspicuously. His swan seemed to have little mechanical feet, swimming ridiculously fast under the untroubled surface of St. Saens' melody. Yet the swan seemed to stay in place, perhaps even to lose ground. James could picture it sinking. The rehearsal bogged onward.

"Mr. Baxter, I have the distinct impression that you are rushing the tempo."

"It's true. I'll confess. I was thinking about taking another breath, and wondering if I would get to the measure where I could, and then I was thinking about these young people who will be waiting to be married and then to get on with their lives. Young people are not patient nowadays. They like their music peppy. This stuff is slow and sticky. I am getting old and tired as we play it. Osteoporosis. Hemorrhoids. Alzheimer's. You name it, I'm getting it."

"Mr. Baxter, this is unprofessional."

"I am not a professional anymore. I am an amateur. That means I am entitled to enjoy myself when I play. This, Miss Evangeline, whatever it is we are doing here, is not any fun. The word that comes to my mind is 'excruciating.' One's thoughts hasten to the notion of crucifixion. 'Agonizing' is another good word. Flaubert might have been thinking of this rehearsal when he described Emma Bovary's reaction to the rat poison she ate. All that vomiting and screaming in agony. Other examples in literature . . . " James broke off. Perhaps he had been harsh.

Evangeline said nothing. Her lips compressed into a fine pencil line, she gathered her music together, fit it carefully into a folder and departed. Her feet made no sound, but she seemed to list from port to starboard alternately—James was suddenly reminded of a similarly very silent person, his third grade teacher, whom he had not thought of in many years, Mrs. Harris, who would stalk an unsuspecting student from behind if the child were violating a rule, talking to a neighbor perhaps, then seize the miscreant by the shoulders and begin shaking. First, books would fall out of the desk, then the desk itself would fall away, leaving only the dangling and still shaking (and shaken) child. Mrs. Harris had a limp—this made her approach more terrible, more awe-inspiring. Evangeline had swayed like Mrs. Harris as she made her exit. As a parting gesture of his own, James played the birdcall from Prokofiev's *Peter and the Wolf*. It was rough and uneven, but certainly lively.

"The bird, Miss Evangeline. I offer you the bird," James said to himself in the same tone of voice as he had used to ask if the flute were a difficult instrument to play. And suddenly, she was back, rocking toward him, his third grade teacher, Mrs. Harris, listing from Gee to Haw, moving toward him inexorably—James could feel his heart thumping wildly—imagine the charge of any horrible wild beast—but then it was Evangeline, who had forgotten her purse in the front row of pews.

*

That evening James was enjoying a rerun of *Law and Order*, one in which Sam Waterson becomes progressively more and more indignant, his voice cracking and his hair sprouting indignant cowlicks. "Justice," James said to himself, not for the first time, "justice, justice, justice." James had had a few glasses of wine and a half of a frozen pizza. It was not a dark and stormy night, but a knock came at the door anyway.

Margaret rushed in the door and burst into tears. Several moths accompanied her and began to flutter raggedly about the room. James wondered if his leaving the porch light on had attracted Margaret, too. One moth, a large black one, flew in circles around James while Margaret continued to weep. He grabbed at it and discovered to his surprise that he had captured it inside his hand. He opened the door and tossed it into the night. It flew, unscathed, away. While he was inclined to perform the same operation with Margaret, James noticed the credits rolling on the TV. Enough of justice. He turned off the TV with the remote and offered Margaret a box of tissues. To give himself something to do during the extensive nose-blowing which followed, James poured Margaret a glass of wine which she drank down like Gatorade—James was at a loss to do anything other than pour her another.

"Mrs. Marmaduke has quit; she has resigned," Margaret blurted, beginning to sob again, but not before drinking most of the second glass of wine. James poured himself another while Margaret dabbed and sniffed *poco a poco dimuendo al niente*.

"She said you were terribly rude, Mr. Baxter."

"It was a musicians' tiff, Margaret. You've been to music school. She wanted to play loud. I wanted to play soft. Or something along those lines. I don't remember. You know that piece, the 'Meditation' from *Thais*?"

Margaret nodded, and having finished her wine, looked expectantly at her former teacher. James poured some from his glass into hers.

"It is really, if you will pardon the expression, a piece of sh.., all right, of doo doo. It is mawkish and sentimental and would sound best played on the upside-down violin by Heathcliff while Wuthering Heights disappears in a mudslide." James refreshed both their glasses.

"I told Mandolin I found it distasteful."

"Evangeline?"

"Yes, a lovely woman. And her banjo, too. She took it personally. Besides, I can't play that piece. I am out of practice. You must hold a high F sharp until the cows come home and no self-respecting cow would come home under those circumstances. Say, would you like to smoke a joint?"

"Yes, and would you pour me some more of that wine? It isn't very good."

James laughed but Margaret apparently hadn't intended a humorous effect. He rolled a nice tight one with the 1.5-wide cigarette paper he used to blot the moisture on his flute pads, searched the kitchen for a match, found one, lit the thing and took a modest toke before passing it to Margaret. Margaret inhaled professionally. Nobody coughed.

"Roddy and I broke up." This came with rather flat inflexion in the small space between an exhalation and a longer, more urgent draw on the joint. It burned halfway to her fingers. James rescued it

96

and after taking a tiny puff, pinched it out with wine-wetted fingers.

"Enough for now," he said.

"Roddy and I broke up because he said Evangeline Marmuduke was stupid and that my Balinesian chant was stupid and that you were a stupid idea."

"At least I'm an idea, not merely stupid." James had run out of wine, wondered whether he should uncork another bottle. He was pretty sure there was another bottle somewhere.

"I want to call you James. Is that okay, Mr. Baxter?"

"Yes, Margaret, you can call me James."

"Thank you, Mr. Baxter." Margaret looked at her wine glass. It, too, was empty. The kitchen clock, which produced the songs of birds on the hour, offered a metallic blue jay. It was ten o'clock, an odd time for blue jays. After the interruption of the jay, the silence deepened. Time had definitely slowed down. James was afraid he was going to become philosophical—it was that time in the high.

"I have an idea," he said decidedly.

"What?" Margaret suddenly seemed hopeful. Her voice was no longer flat. There was color in her cheeks.

"I have forgotten. No. Yes. I have it again. A flute lesson. Let's have a flute lesson. I'll teach you to play the 'Meditation' from *Thais*."

"I don't have a flute, but I have a toothbrush in my purse."

"Margaret, I'll loan you a flute. I don't brush my students' teeth, I give them flute lessons."

And so James produced a flute, assembled it, and gave it to Margaret.

"Now, here is the flute, and here is the music, fresh from Miss Dobro's no doubt pirated software. There is an introduction missing but don't concern yourself. Are you rusty, too?"

"I'm thirsty, and I have the munchies, but I can think of something better to do before the munchies."

"Never mind that, my dear. First you must play."

James remembered Margaret's hearty tone as if her last lesson had been only yesterday. Now she seemed exhausted. A faint hoot came from the flute.

"Big breaths."

"Yeth, and I'm only ten yearth old."

"Margaret. You have committed humor. You used to have a lisp, you know."

"I know. It was adorable. But let's do something else."

"Would you rather play 'The Swan?'

"No, Mr. James." Margaret handed him the flute. She was a pretty girl in the bloom of her youth. James thought, why not? He had only to put the flute away. He played the opening phrase of the "Meditation" on his way to the case he had left on the kitchen table. It sounded rather good. He walked back to the music stand in the living room. He played the second phrase. Quite lovely, really. By the time he had got to the end of the piece, his high notes were exquisite in the diminuendos, his low notes rich and bell-like. He hadn't sounded this good in years. It couldn't possibly be the dope.

He found Margaret at the kitchen table. Margaret had found and uncorked the second bottle of wine. There were ice cubes in her glass. She had also found and finished the joint.

"That was pretty."

"So are you."

"I'm not going to marry Roddy." Here the clock broke in. Another blue jay. Time warp, James thought.

"Perhaps you will."

Margaret was chasing her ice cubes around in a circle with her finger.

"I've changed my mind about doing something else, too."

"Ah, ever the bridesmaid. Oh, sorry. And I'm afraid I've stretched the metaphor to the breaking point, anyway."

"No, you're saying that you seldom get the opportunity to fuck your students."

"Margaret, please. Besides, I was the one who played Massenet while Rome burned."

"Now you're getting all weird. Oh, I get it. You had the music-munchies and lost your window of opportunity."

"It would have been revenge sex anyway."

"Revenge sex can be awesome."

"This is not a conversation I anticipated having with you when you walked into my studio back at B.B. Givings."

Margaret took a final drink of her wine water. "You'd rather remember me as a sweet little girl with a lisp?"

"Yep."

"How much do I owe you for the lesson, then?"

"It's on the house."

*

98

As it turned out, Margaret did marry Roddy, only the wedding was in August, and while James was invited, he was unable to attend. He was busy house hunting in Ohio where he had found another visiting position at a small college where he would teach poetry as well as fiction, a prospect he found very attractive, because he secretly wrote poetry and, in fact, had often fantasized about retiring from the world and only wearing white.

After the wedding, Margaret kept in touch. She became interested in playing the flute again, and in a few years was playing for weddings and receptions herself. Her organizational skills served her well, and on a typical summer weekend, she was booking four or five different engagements a day, choosing for herself only the choice ones.

Margaret and Roddy divorced after a year and a half, there being no children—and Roddy was allergic to pet dander so there were no coon cats or poodles to bicker over. Margaret began to send James musicians' haiku she claimed to have composed herself: "Squeaking and squawking / All eyes roll to the heavens / The clarinet speaks"— "Pit orchestra gig / Days and nights become as one / I have no damn life." James replied with haiku written by his own students: "Life is like bowling / When your hand is in the holes / It is real sweaty"— "The tail of incense / In the burner, left unburned / Looks like a fish turd." James was proud of his students and abandoned his Emily Dickinson fantasies—began rather to fancy himself in a ZZ Top beard, wrote poems in very long lines and sent them to journals where, occasionally, one would be published but go unread. He considered buying a pickup truck with a gun rack.

Then, while James was attending an MLA convention in an eastern city, and Margaret was on tour with a Jan Svankmajer puppet musical, the two arranged to meet in the bar of a large hotel.

"Remember Evangeline?" Margaret asked. She had kissed James lightly on his cheek and ordered a martini. She didn't look like a musician, James decided.

"This is an academic convention,' he told her. "Do you think I look like an academic?"

"She's the musical director for the biggest Baptist church in the city. She even produces recording projects. Wait till you hear my Celtic Christmas CD."

"Academics are very predictable," James said. "They would insist on producing an Islamic Christmas CD."

"They keep changing the puppets. We play the same music, but the puppets change. It's depressing."

"So it's that old dilemma: old music; new puppets."

"What?" Margaret tossed off her martini and looked annoyed.

"No, really. Do you think I look like an academic?" James was wearing a tweed sport jacket with leather elbow patches.

"Mostly you look like somebody from Ohio."

"Let's go up to my room."

"Another drink first, okay?" Margaret had another martini and James had a glass of white wine for old time's sake.

"How can you tell if a viola is playing out of tune?" Margaret asked.

"The bow is moving. What's the definition of perfect pitch?"

"You told me that joke before. Something about a dumpster."

Margaret and James went up to his room, taking an elevator filled to capacity with unsmiling people dressed in tweed and corduroy surreptitiously reading each other's name tags. The room had a nice view.

"I guess it's time," Margaret said.

"Right ho," James said.

"Right ho?"

Afterward, they promised each other they would meet again soon. Six months later, Margaret married again, this time an official of the musicians' union. Before that, James sent her several of his long-lined poems but received no reply.

*

Late one evening, a few years later, James found himself writing Margaret a long letter, one in which he rambled on about a clipped newspaper photo he had come across that day, cleaning out his desk. It was taken back in the old days of the B. B. Givings Community Music School, and it was of him and Margaret when she was just beginning to learn the flute. It had been taken by a newspaper photographer doing a story on the school. James had written several single-spaced pages which he hoped were wistful and a little funny, and in which he hinted that they should meet sometime soon. But when he came back to the keyboard with a refreshed glass of wine, he noticed the photo again: There was Margaret, a chubby little girl, with her red hair and her flute—and there was James, holding a finger in front of his lips, showing Margaret how to blow and feel the air with her finger, but it looked as if he were saying, "Hush. Be still."

James looked at his letter and then at the photo. His younger self seemed to be looking out at him. James sighed, marked his text, and punched delete. He took his evening glass of wine with him to sit on the front porch where several moths were circling raggedly, thumping against the porch light. He thought of the night of Margaret's *Thais* flute lesson. Had there been a moon for them to stand under when he walked her to her car? He couldn't remember. Was the flute a difficult instrument to play? "Hush," he said to himself. "Be still."

REMBRANDT'S NOSE
Philadelphia, 1975, 2002

II

At home I made myself a peanut butter and jelly sandwich and had a glass of milk. This child's meal calmed me. It was early afternoon of a day that hadn't been wasted—I felt this in spite of my student's phone call, canceling our lesson. I could take the train to Germantown and surprise Anna. I could play with clay while I waited for her to finish her classes—pinch pots, little slab boxes—there was a shelf there of little figures, creatures, frogs and mice I had made, waiting to be glazed. What, I wondered, would an adult do?

I went outside and discovered that the day had transformed itself. It was cloudy and a ragged breeze was blowing up from the river. Scraps of newspaper noticed it. Nobody was on the street, maybe because a storm was brewing or because everybody but me had something constructive to do. I could practice. I was memorizing the Karg-Elert *Caprices*, and was up to number eleven, *Auberst geschwind und locker*, in F sharp minor. This undertaking, I decided, did not complement peanut butter.

I had wandered around the corner to the other side of the boarded-up elementary school when there was a powerful clap of thunder and lightning flash—not the shape of lightning that we can enjoy from a distance, but an abrupt illumination—I thought I had been struck and I stumbled up the brick steps of the school entrance. Rain came down like a solid object, rushing and seething. My ears rang with thunder and rain and with a foreground of sudden drippings and runnels—I had backed up the school steps as far as I could and I was standing before the boarded door, which I realized wasn't really closed. It had been pushed or broken open and stood a few inches ajar. The boards were only wedged into place. A lot of water was beginning to leak down from above me so I forced my way past the boards and the old faded, unreadable sign.

I immediately recognized the source of the neighborhood's characteristic smell, a vast damp moldy looming stink. And when I turned around to look into the darkness, there at some distance—it was a big room—was a candle on a table and, behind it, his arms on the tabletop in the same pose as Saskia in silverpoint, was the young Rembrandt himself, his hair standing out in curls, half in darkness, chiaroscuro. I stared and the candle flickered, and the image of Rembrandt transformed itself into Mary's boyfriend, Stan Kershenski. No question about it. A wild-haired guy with a limp. He looked pretty much the same as in the days when he was supposedly making his living making candles, except for the hair.

For a few moments we just looked at each other, long enough, I guess, for Stan to see that I was alone. He waved me into the dark room, warning me to watch my feet. There were bricks and cinder blocks scattered about, but my eyes had adjusted and there was a little light still coming from the door. Stan's story came with a lot of cracked eggs—he had watched too many TV cartoons with his brain pickled—for some reason, he was hiding out. Lenny was after him. Mighty Mouse was after him, too. He was waiting for something or somebody. He gave me a twenty and told me to get him pork rinds and RC Cola—as much as I could buy. He was very specific about that.

*

Anna didn't seem particularly disappointed when I declined to go to the next drawing class. I told her that drawing from the model was too hard for me, and that I was embarrassed that Mary, someone I actually knew, however casually, was the model. I would stay home and practice Karg-Elert. I was up to number thirteen, *Leichthin, anmutig, wie 2 Flöten*. And I did for a while. It's one of the few slow K-E Caprices. You have to change the sound to give the effect of two different players. I was really involved and didn't think the knocking I heard was at my door until it got louder. I put the flute on the stand on the little table and opened the door, expecting maybe my neighbor Tommy with some kind of complaint—he didn't mind me practicing, he just liked to rag me about the music I played. But this was Stan.

"Are you going to tell on me?"

"Stan, come . . . " He pushed past me and I shut the door. His eyes didn't look right—the pupils were dilated, probably not from a visit to the ophthalmologist.

"*Are* you going to tell on me?"

"Stan, I haven't said a word to anyone. It's been a week."

He sat down on the bottom stairs of the spiral staircase. I didn't much like that—it was my special place. Now his back was covered. I started putting the flute away.

"Mary's driving me to North Carolina tomorrow—her sister's got a farm. And I got to thinking. This is your last chance to get me."

Stan's hands were shaking a little and his voice was tight, but then he always seemed excited. All I had to defend myself was a flute, now half in the case.

"It's been a week, Stan. Nobody's been around. I haven't said anything to anybody—and if I did, it would look like I was involved."

Stan kept shaking his head, going through the choreography of serious thought.

"Mary said something about you—she said you and Anna were on the outs—that you had been hanging around, trying to get into her. . . . "

"Not me. Hey look. I'm practicing my music." I waved at the music stand and had to catch Karg-Elert on the way down. Our kitchen was a very small room and whatever Stan had been smoking was probably seeping out into the air.

"All right. All right. She didn't say nothing. I just got to thinking— she did say you and Anna weren't doing good. . . . " He looked at me expectantly. His eyes had begun to react to the light in the room. Maybe he wasn't completely stoned.

"I don't know. She talks to Mary. Not to me. You want a beer?"

*

Hendrickje died of the plague in 1663—Rembrandt's son, Titus, died of the plague in 1668. Rembrandt himself died the next year. His last self-portraits are of a man whose fat and puffy face had grown milder, its surfaces weathered and softened, but the eyes are still alive. He couldn't help painting himself seeing. His nose had begun to fill up with air—if he'd had a few more years, it would have become a hot air balloon and drifted out of the frame.

I bought Stan one more batch of groceries before he disappeared, and Anna spent the last two weeks of August with Mary "and a friend" she wrote me, on that farm in North Carolina—maybe the FBI *was* after Stan. I was in Italy with a group of traveling musicians, playing Puccini and Berio. I made my way back to Philadelphia with one line of Italian, "*Questo traino va a Milano?*"

It was during the last few months that we were together in Philadelphia that we heard about Mary's accident. She had been crushed under a tractor. Anna went back to North Carolina, and before she returned home, I had left to take a job with a Southern orchestra. Still, Anna spent most of that year with me in Nashville— we took a long time to do what we were doing. We had stopped having sex but, to the end, we behaved like lovers, holding hands and nuzzling each other. It seems strange to me now, but it didn't then—or maybe it was just that sex was the least of what was going on, what was falling apart.

Falling apart. She left me the little falling-apart book with "The Naughty Child" and "Saskia Sitting Up in Bed," and "Young Man Pulling a Rope." I leafed through it in the late hours when I knew I wasn't going to get to sleep. I still found the magical nests of tangled lines, but it was the titles, those simple straightforward titles that were reassuring for me in times that weren't. Above the young man with the rope there's a bell, but you don't get to see it. I imagine he's waiting for it to peal, to ring just once. He's always waiting.

Then I lost the little book in one of my frequent moves. It was one of the things I think I would have tried to save first from a burning house, and I did replace it with two large volumes containing all the drawings and etchings—but it wasn't the same.

LISTENING
Nashville, 2002

There's thunder and sporadic rain and a single robin is still singing and Harold has been dead three years now. There was finally a memorial service in Philadelphia and C and I were there. The gathering was on and off and then on again, finally scheduled at the Ethical Society where Harold and I had performed so often. Chris and Jack were there and Harold's ex-wife and his old friend and roommate Alice. Chris played a recording of a piece for viola and orchestra that Harold had written. Chris's daughter (I remember her as a tiny girl—but that was long ago, before his first wife found the twigs in his underwear and divorced him)—Chris's daughter, transformed in the length of a single sentence into a beautiful grown woman, sang several of Harold's art songs. I played the piece Harold had written for me, "Music for a Poem," and before I played it, I talked to the gathered audience and told them some of my Harold stories.

7/4/95

Dear James,

The morning has begun its own quiet celebration. It is 6:30. I have opened the window. There is a gentle breeze floating in—floating out, a bit of Korngold: the Violin Concerto. It is too early for the usual insults from traffic; Philadelphia is always slow to rise on holidays. One can actually hear the gloved approbation of wings. (The Poet and Pigeon Overture*)*

I say a "bit of Korngold": I put six discs into the JVC and selected the random mode. After a few minutes, after a few tracks from Ligeti, Korngold, Boulez, Rachmaninov, Prokofiev, Barber—I feel as if I had rediscovered the jukebox. Something else, too: I remembered a dinner which Anna made (after one of our lessons on Green Street), rice & curry—an extravagant number of condiments, each in its own little bowl, each one a sensational delight. The two of you were very kind to me.

There are stories I tell and stories I don't tell. The Dalawa is not one for a memorial service. Now, I have done the Dalawa with Harold. Understand. This is a religious exercise—the naked soul calling out to God in many names. Calling the name Allah. These are only men in this darkened room. The women are someplace else, singing like Botticelli's angels. We men are not angels. We are shuffling feet and

106

novelty song lyrics. I danced around in the dark and listened to Chris writing the book on smelly feet. "I have smelly feet. You have smelly feet. All God's children have smelly feet."

But smelly feet or not, I never talked to Brahms as Harold once told me he did. Did Harold know I resented his visions, that I wished Brahms had talked to me? Jean Pierre Rampal talked to me during a break in a rehearsal once. We were both tired as hell. I of the conductor and he of playing the same CPE Bach concerto all his life. In D minor. Who cares about conductors? They are all worthless. I asked him why he didn't play the G major concerto and he said it was too *tres difficile*. True, I commiserated. Now both Rampal and Harold are dead.

"I was astounded," he would tell me about something that happened in a lesson, or about a performance he had heard recently. Harold was always being astounded. He often walked out on performances, amazed at the incompetence and stupidity of the performers. He did not plan to find fault—his innocence in that respect was powerful. And he did champion a few. He sent me a tape of the flutist for whom the Danish composer Carl Nielson wrote his flute concerto. The playing was very fine, but the guy played with no vibrato. This, I can tell you, is not conventional in today's world of flute playing. There is a story about Pablo Casals, addressing his orchestra during a rehearsal, intoning in a voice quivering like a flag in the wind, "No vibrato, no vibrato."

9/21/97
Dear James,
I'm starting my morning with coffee and several discs of the sturdy Mr. E. Carter. Piano Concerto, Variations for Orchestra, Concerto for Orchestra. 3 Occasions, Chamber Pieces. *Followed by* Pelleas & Melisande, *and no doubt my noon nap.*

I'm medicated to something resembling normalcy, and scheduled to return to work Oct 1ˢᵗ.

"No vibrato, no vibrato." This is the moment of amazement for me, the visit of the Dalawa. All the hidden imps of the spirit awakened, poking at the various chakras with their tiny pitchforks. God speaks. "No Vibrato." The words elongated. Each vowel (pronounced in the

European style) a paean of quivering, vibrating motion. Here are the elementary particles, blinking in and out of existence. Here is the essential contradiction, the necessary koan, the obstacle over which we must trip and begin to fall, and in that fall, falling, we may measure our lives because time is elastic, and even a second will break into as many pieces as the world can contain—I'm standing in a rather shabby room, the one used for meetings and small concerts for the Ethical Society, and many of Harold's friends are gathered here. My old friend Chris, so tired now, it seems, has put all this together, hauling the speakers and sound equipment from Wilmington, where he still teaches (but no longer sleeps with, I would venture to guess) his many students. Chris's hair is gone. He seems to have worried it away, follicle by follicle, but the wrinkles in his brow are lively, cheered by the opportunity to commiserate.

"Our Harold is gone," he beams. Then his expression darkens. "But not now," he grasps my hand in both of his, "not a word now." He returns to his speakers, tripping over some wires and pulling out the connections. He is in his element.

10/23/97

Dear James,

Well, I've lost your letter amid the debris on my desk. Some days are clearer than others. This is not one of them. I forgot my appointment with Dr. Perkheimer. Now I'm so depressed I can't seem to leave the apartment so I called in sick to work. Easier to say "sick" than frigging freaked out. Some days I wonder if all this medicine is really doing me any good. My voices are relatively quiet—which is good. But today I'm very nervous, for some reason. A blanket over my head sounds like a very handsome idea. A cave.

I have chosen to tell the congregation about the time Harold showed up at a reading I gave in Bryn Mawr looking like he had fallen off a train—it was nearly that: he got off at the wrong stop and ran the rest of the way. I decided not to tell them about the time he offered the toast at my wedding in what was apparently fluent Arabic.

3/7/98

Dear James,

I've just been laid off. 18 years at the vitamin gig. Monday down to the

108

unemployment office. (And no, I don't think this is a poem.)
Bit of Rachmaninov on CDs keeping me company.
My medications seem to keep me afloat.
I feel as silly as Satie. At least he could write.
Dr. Perkheimer would be happy to see me getting out more.
One of his projects is to make me go to a bookstore, order some coffee
& read awhile.
I had a single espresso, took 2 swallows and beat it out of there. He
says rather dryly: Try again. Time for my nap.

I'm sure Harold was astounded at my wedding—anything ordinary would often seem quite otherwise to him. He would have told the story of it himself—and to whom? Probably Mike—those were his gay years. Mike is one face missing from this memorial service, this gathering of old friends. Lovers. There was one branch that chose to break rather than bend. They so often do.

That was a time in Harold's life I know very little about. I was earning my single-parent merit badge with an infant. The old lady who lived across the street from me and baby, who provided childcare during my concerts and rehearsals, taught me enough of the basics to permit the child to survive. Now that I think about it, I can remember about as much of Harold's life then as I can of my own. He had been mixed up with a playwright, a woman of some accomplishment, I think. I visited him when I was still married to Gwyn—he was living in a large house in West Philadelphia with this woman. Her name was Dorothy. And there was an entourage, several people, a dozen, some of them actually living in the house.

I can remember a brilliant morning, with lines and splashes of sunlight obscuring the shabby furniture of the living room. Gwyn and I sat with Harold while he described something (his life with Dorothy, a play, a concert?) in *medias res*. Harold was not in the habit of providing exposition. I have never grasped the story of his childhood (other than he was abandoned by his mother) for the same reason. That day Gwyn and I sat stiffly, wishing for coffee, in a scrap yard of sun swatches, breakfast noises coming from the kitchen— strangers were walking past, some from the house, some come from elsewhere—no one offered us anything.

I had brought Gwyn to Philadelphia to show her off to my friends. The first thing I discovered was that she refused to speak in public.

It was the beginning of my awakening. Who is this woman, my friends wondered. Who is this woman, I wondered along with them. In various degrees of embarrassment, we concluded that she was content to sit in rooms, gaze out the windows, answer direct questions in monosyllables. Harold, however, did not seem embarrassed by Gwyn's presence—he hardly seemed to notice her. His narrative was rich, if impenetrable.

He only became evasive when I brought up the concerto he had been working on for me. It should be understandable that working on a play, *Orphans of the Opera*, did not fit handily with the composition of a flute concerto. His work on the play seemed to have been going on, on the one hand, for years, but on the other, he seemed to have just begun to imagine it. There were readings of it which had just taken place or which were about to take place—it was difficult for me to tell. At one point Dorothy herself trailed majestically through the room in something purple.

"Bring me my paper," she commanded without looking at anyone, a point guard delivering a behind-the-back pass. Harold scuttled into the next room, nearly colliding with a more efficient flunky who was bringing, of all things, the daily comics pages. Dorothy was an important woman. I had known Harold to take up with a scrawny pianist in the past—Diane was an important woman, too, now that I think of it. I suppose that passion cannot be important enough.

And there I was with my Gwyn, beginning to feel monumentally trivial. Sure enough, before the lovely sun splotches had dimmed, Harold bid us a distracted adieu and Gwyn and I went on to a meeting with a psychologist Anna had found for us. During this meeting, Gwyn came to some profound understanding of her relationship with her father, indeed, both her parents, and wept for an hour, resolving to reinvest her passion and spirit into our relationship. A day later, as we were driving home, I mentioned the epiphany to her and she denied even shedding one tear. Seizure of awareness, indeed.

7/15/98

Dear James,

This morning, I took the elevator down to the first floor to collect my (hoped-for) letters. I could have walked as it's only four flights but it's over a hundred degrees, and exceptionally humid. And I am old: life has been unkind, and I'm tired. At the mailbox there were several young people

110

in various states of sex, undress, hair length—all sweetly sweated-up this
their moving day. I found it all rather pleasant, except for the fact that
their neatly packed stuff, hundreds of boxes & unidentifiable black bags
had completely blocked access to the mailboxes—I came back upstairs.
They had addressed me as 'Sir.' It was more than I'd hoped for.

Shortly after our visit to Philadelphia, my apprenticeship in childcare for the single parent began. As a careful reader might well have expected, Gwyn and I brought a child into the world, separated, and divorced in a trice. During this time Harold did not call or write. What then? Mornings. The weather moving from west to east. The child, learning to walk, falls on the stone patio, gets two black eyes. I am amazed to watch the healing take place. The old woman across the street tells me that children will fall down. Extraordinary.

Now a sudden call from Harold. He has broken his leg dancing. He describes an evening of frolic I would not have chosen for a story involving his particular, rather fastidious character. He is dancing with someone who is an old friend, not Dorothy, but another one of those characters from the missing exposition, perhaps Alice. He describes the sound of the leg breaking. After a while, I can see the light in the room, hear the ambiance. The leg breaking might be my own.

I tell him I have learned about the miracle of healing. He is noncommittal. I am teaching my child to ride a tricycle. I have taped blocks of wood to the pedals so that his chubby little legs will reach. Outside, in the parking lot of the apartment complex where I now live alone in several rooms carpeted in rich brown shag—the color of shit, really, but fine for the child when he tumbles down—I am pushing him around, my hands holding his feet to the pedals. He likes this, but when I let go, he can't seem to get the knack of doing it himself. As frustrating (try crawling around on a blacktop parking lot on your knees, hands working the pedals of a tiny tricycle)—as exhausting as this is for me, he bursts into tears and tantrums when I decide to take him back into our brown-carpeted womb.

Harold's broken leg encourages our communication and I receive several scenes from plays which I cannot decipher. One is set in Frederick the Great's palace of Sans Souci and is concerned with a long poker game involving Fred, young CPE Bach, old Quantz, and another character who may or may not be the visiting Johann Sebastian. *Orphans of the Opera* seems to involve Yniold from *Pelleas* and Hop Hop from *Wozzick*. Children, of course, often play at incomprehensible games. I am playing games with my own child which would fill Harold with that same amazement he finds at concerts and lessons and my wedding.

9/18/98
Dear James,

Verdi's Macbeth *is on the radio—Muti at La Scala. A silly and beautiful piece. I drift in and out.*

Thanks for the nice letter & the gift of your poems. And your kind words to me.

The road back seems terribly long even though much of last year—I have no recollection. Some of my medications cause some memory loss, others trigger a craving for carbohydrates. Now I can't remember why I'm getting fat.

Then the leg healed and perhaps the child even learned to ride his tricycle. I remember dragging a magnet of the type used to raise sunken outboard motors across my brown pile carpet to find the screw that had fallen and disappeared while I was repairing a flute—the tiny thing was essential—the instrument lay in pieces for a week while I waited for the mail-order magnet to arrive. It was a triumph of good luck for me to find that screw clinging to the magnet, along with the ferrous detritus of the previous inhabitants of the brown-bottomed room.

In this next foggy passage of time, Harold's letters begin to change—they seem more urgent; he might be writing to himself. And mine, I don't know. . . . This time is like the old days for us, when we sat together in the kitchen in the house on Delancey Street, drinking until dawn. My life is changing, certainly another story—I have met my C—and Harold (he will tell me this later) has been thrown out of the house in West Philly. Who was this woman who threw him out? What was his transgression? I don't need the tiny devils to tell me. She is prideful, an artist, and Harold (who cannot hold his liquor) has reminded her of some awful truth, that she was born in Joplin, Missouri where her father still operates a funeral parlor, or that she mispronounces a common word, ruff for roof, perhaps.

Might it have been some sexual thing? No, that is to come. He is wretched. Some friend, Ron or Randy, or Raul, not Chris, who is making a new family with his twiggy student in Delaware, some single friend has made a place for Harold in the reed-making room, or the storage closet, or what passes for the library; and Harold is wretched. He wanders the streets. Forgive me for not providing the details. Mike takes him in. (When I was a young man, cars slowed as I walked the streets of Philadelphia—was it just my youth, a general blooming of sorts, or was there something in the walk, a visual pheromone? The cars would creep along and then drive away, the next step in the dance missing.) I was not wandering. There was always some place to go, so I did not have any of those experiences which might permit me to provide a paragraph linking Dorothy to Mike.

5:30 AM Philly June & Clear—I'm walking back from the Wawa on Locust street carrying a half gallon of milk, two packs of Camels & feeling quite pleased with myself for having noticed the moon. It is huge! A four-quartered Opera sung on rice paper. And lopsided, but that, by design—like the self-deprecating, crooked grin of someone who knows the value of their own looks/charms. And the sky! A playful slap with its challenging, yet-to-be-identified blue. I try to imprint it on my memory, try to figure out how best it might be described—"Hey! Can I get a cigarette off ya?" I decide this has a blond, flannel, stonewashed, pre-disastered, sandpapered-denim-crotch, thing going for it. I shake one out for him and as he takes it his fingers lightly brush my hand. He stares at the cigarette for a moment. "Match?" I offer. "No," he says, tucking it as clerks do with their pencils behind an ear. He puts a hand onto my shoulder, looks me straight in the eyes, and says, "This is for later . . . much later." I almost laugh. It's the pause: very Pinteresque. Instead I return to him what I hope will be read as a perfection of confusions, even though my shoulder has not only understood, it's telling me that it's very interested, and inquiring into the feasibility of our breakdancing. (I've been celibate for two and one half yrs.) Still, there's enough blood and fear left in my brain to say, "No," to his "You're not looking for anybody, are you?" Already, his eyes have moved on. His hand follows, quick to give a 'thumbs-up' to the BMW convertible passing by. He decides to chase it, sprinting away without so much as a curt nod. At the corner the car stops. He catches up. They talk. He gets in and slams the door, an act echoed at my refrigerator. I feel as if someone has sandblasted my last nerve. Looking out the window I see that the moon has gone, that blue has gone, that guy . . . I need music. Beethoven!

(Schnabel's 1937 recording of the "Diabelli" Variations) Some charms can be captured and will never, ever fade.

This is what I know. Mike lived in a little house in Fishtown. He had a wife and family (high school-age children) and an extended family, all living in the same neighborhood. Everyone seemed to think this business was temporary, a digression, this taking in of the musician, lately playwright. It was to be Harold's longest stable relationship. Mike collected ducks, ceramic ducks, ivory ducks, carved wooden ducks, crystal ducks, plastic ducks. Those long years, he was Harold's friend and lover. But he did not care about literature or painting or classical music. And when Harold became a burden, Mike threw him out. Harold spoke of him bitterly as the "Prince of Duckness."

It is raining and humid again. Mimi & Rodolfo are getting back together again though it's just to say addio. *I use the rain as an excuse not to look for work today. (It will mess up my hair, my suit, my shoes) What's one more day? I will go out: the book I ordered from Jos. Fox has arrived. They called. Fetching it makes me feel . . . responsible. Mimi is about to croak & my eyes are dry. (It used to mess me up.) It is Rodolfo—now he's a mess, screaming out those high G sharps. Thank God her name wasn't FIFI! Yeah, I know. Go Look For A Job. Now.*

Harold began to paint after the time he spent with Dorothy. The first time I realized that he was painting was when he asked me for a photograph of myself. I procrastinated but Anna supplied him with one. Then he gave me a small portrait—I no longer have the portrait but it was a good likeness of me. In it I have a rather Trotsky-like beard and my hair is long. This is the James of those days in the big house on Delancey, another stranger passing me on the street. The colors were the best part, hearty browns and blues, and I began to enjoy the little portrait when I discovered that no one saw me in it.

Most of the paintings Harold did thereafter were made up of tiny Seurat dots. And to my taste, the mostly pastel colors he employed were unsatisfactory, even trivial. I probably let him in on my lack of interest in some careless way. Certainly Harold did not write to me about his painting except to say that the dots took very long to paint. C admired his work and especially *The Red Lady,* an enormous unfinished twisting torso of a woman. Twelve feet high, it barely fit into our van. Of course,

Harold gave it to her. It moves about in our houses from one storage room to the next—there have been no walls large enough for it.

During the Tornado Watch James' book arrived. I read it through, excitedly, pronounced him a grownup, scribbled off something and handed it to the girl playing mailman. Will I always be this child? Will I always be?

Now I'm telling the gathering about the piece I am going to play, "Music for a Poem," and about the time when Harold lived with me and Anna and two other couples in the house on Delancey Street. I have decided not to read them the poem, which Harold chose from the many that I wrote in that year. The one that Harold chose was particularly terrible, and I argued with him about it some years later in an exchange of letters—until I realized that I had insulted him. I in my paroxysms of modesty had managed only to criticize and impugn his judgment. No matter, the other poems from which he might have chosen were terrible, too. I'm merely being prideful when I deny both those young men (for whom the cars still slowed down) their youthful enthusiasm. Harold's piece is for solo flute and I'll play it in a moment. Along with a few of Harold's songs which Chris's daughter will sing, it will be the only live music. The rest will come, muffled and streaked with sonic dust, from Chris's ancient sound system, one which I'm certain he would never consider replacing.

At the zoo, two cats: one's asleep, and the other pads over and just slaps the shit outta his cellmate, and I sez: 'Been there.'

Now I've begun to play and I'm immediately acquainted with the dimensions, the space, of the hall, all its dusty reaches—I'm tuned to the listening audience, their shiftings on the folding wooden chairs, their breathings—there is a kind of chronic undertow of breathing in this hall, this space of air filled with the surfaces of humans, some of them weeping. I must breathe, myself, and each breath allows me to elevate, or to lower myself into Harold's composition, which is made up of slow descending semitones which are themselves decorated at the space of one or more octaves with rapid semitones—the piece seems to be constantly slowing itself down. I can hear Harold finding its notes on the piano in the great room back in the house on Delancey Street. The effect is like listening to birdcalls. In particular, the wood thrush.

Silences created by the spacing of the calls have as much an effect on me as the call itself. When Harold was working at the piano, the silence was the working of his mind, or perhaps he was listening. In the forest, that silence is another kind of mind working. This is the mind of God, I will say the name, and that is the silence that has taken over Harold now, no longer a pause between sporadic efforts. Still, eternity itself is a pause, and something may rise from it. This music was perhaps most true to itself when he was trying it, when it was separated from itself by days and by nights when we sat and drank in the yellow-lit kitchen with the cats fighting under the huge restaurant stove. Now as I play it, those wood thrush silences have closed in and the most precious part of the music, its becoming, has been framed within these commas, my breathing in. The flute is an out-breath; I am an in-breath. And, like elementary particles, we exchange our identities. The more I become myself, the less time I exist in the world, in the room with its wood and its human surfaces and the hidden thoughts, the grieving, the listening, the not-listening.

Midnight walking. Everything familiar's been dissolved. I'm thinking Hollywood got it right—the fog, the mist, the huge budget for fireflies. Somewhere out there in the wet grass, Oberon, Titania, Puck and the rude mechanicals await cues. But the mood is savaged by the barking and snarling of unseen dogs, and I've become paralyzed with a paperboy's fears. Peter says, "Come on, they won't hurt you." I'd forgotten he was there, as I'd forgotten why we were there. I never could quite get a handle on the guy. Peter once told me that there would come a day in which I wouldn't need to write music. That's always haunted me.

The music comes to its end—music is always ending. What happens this time? Applause? Perhaps this is the difference between a memorial service and a funeral. Applause. I smile at the gathered company and find my place, put the flute away in its case. I listen carefully and patiently to the sometimes rambling testimony that remains. Later I'll help Chris pack up his gear and some of us will crowd into a booth at a nearby restaurant. We are hungry and tired. The day is going to end in an ordinary way, as most days do.

The Dalawa is a dance, a spiritual exercise, a meeting with God. It seemed a wonderful coincidence that when Harold and I met again after our student years and we came to live together for a season in the big house, we had both developed the same interest in matters spiritual. Harold and Diane and David were already practicing the Dalawa. Harold said that it was a strange experience for him, but that only inflamed my imagination. How had he learned of it? He wouldn't say. It had just happened—as the really important things in life happen—out of the blue.

I had come from a summer in which I had decided that I would spend my life writing a poem, and that it would be a poem of enlightenment. I had confused in my mind the musician's ritual of daily practice with the craft of making a piece of writing. My mornings of writing, however, gave me great satisfaction, and I didn't burden myself by making any choices. I put my pages away as if they were a treasure too splendid to gaze upon.

My poem and the Dalawa were going to ask the same questions of God and would likely receive the same answer. (I was waiting out the necessary probationary period, sitting outside the closed door where the Dalawa was held.) Harold was on the other side with the others. Just as there was a real door between us, there was a door in my overheated imagination, performing the same function. This was the time of Woodstock, of long hair and drugs and if we did not listen to its music then, we would later. It was the time Harold was my flute student and the freelance guru I had found in Wisconsin came to visit us and told Harold that "someday he would not need to write music." There's one genie I wish I hadn't let out of the bottle.

Finally, the door was opened and the Dalawa took me in. I did not sink into a pit nor fly into the heavens. I danced, it is true, and I think I may have seemed some large mantis, moving slowly, trying not to fall off the branch—but nothing changed. I overheard the conversations that men have with God, and they did not sound to me like poems—my fellow supplicants spun in slow circles, their knees bent, a gesture which is to dance like crooning is to song, but in place of song I heard guttural mumbling and animal noises. But for Harold, it was otherwise. He dove, he flew, he cried out to Allah. Perhaps the voices found him then.

We had already been evicted from the big house, but I was still doggedly striving at the Dalawa. Each time I staggered home from it, Anna wrestled with me like Jacob's angel. She had always refused to come to the Dalawa herself. "Why do you do this if it gives you headaches?" Half the tea she had brewed for me splashed out of the cup when she set it down. We had only each other. Diane and David had moved to New Zealand. Harold and his voices had moved to Wilmington.

In the place where I am writing now, there are many trees. Squirrels swarm over them and chew the new limbs, dropping branches carelessly, foolishly into the yard. Something was chewing at us. We were young and strong and even beautiful, but we broke and fell away. Anna and me. Harold. The others, too.

*

Soon the mouse, the midnight mouse will pop up and I'll snap my fingers and it will run back to the stove, slipping in between the space which surrounds the burners. I'll rise, turn knobs, and watch the gas ignite—a quartet of 'poofs'—even though this action has yet to prove itself a deterrent—even though I'm aware that it's quite possible that it is never the same mouse.

*

When I took the flute down from my lips, in the brief moment before the polite applause began, I was shaken from within. The Dalawa struck me once from within my chest, a bass drum roll, violent but brief, like a dog with a snake—just a reminder, perhaps, that mystery continues, even for those who are not chosen.

This performance was no cathartic experience for me—although I could see that many others were moved. Performance itself, even in a time like this, is always a kind of mystery. Harold seems to me now to be as he always has, more of a presence than not. We lived in different cities during the greater part of our friendship. He kept me and most of his friends in a panic over what he might do next, and whether he would ever be able to take care of himself. He told Anna and me, those long years ago in the big house on Delancey Street that wherever we went, he was going to go with us and live with us. We feared he would and feared he wouldn't.

He was probably in love with me in those days. When he withdrew that passionate admiration, and there was merely friendship remaining—in spite of my relief, I think I felt I had lost something of myself. He chain-smoked and he could not hold his liquor. His health frayed constantly. In the last years his vision blurred because of the medication that was supposed to take away the voices. I don't know how much he could read, or whether he could write, or paint, or hope to write or paint. But he always wrote his letters in the same way. (My mother always wrote the same letters, too. First the weather, then the garden, then the neighborhood.)

With Harold it was setting. "I am sitting here listening to . . . " And it would seem to me to be a wonderful thing to be listening to. Then he would go on to his reading, and to ironic comments upon his creative work. And sometimes there would be a few poems or a fragment of a play. He transcribed a Bach violin partita for me, and then, as an afterthought to that effort, did the "Music for a Poem." I played it often, and felt it was mine. Then as I played fewer solo concerts, and the alto flute was sold, I played it no more. The last time was ten years ago, when I also played Harold's *Concerto Variations,* an almost literal retrograde of the Bartok *Violin Concerto* second movement. I wrote about it in *Listening to Mozart.* Harold wanted to write collaboratively about the experiences of my Great Great Uncle Sylvester Marion Jones and his *Spirit Autobiography.* Harold and C and James should write alternating chapters, he suggested. We just never got around to it.

I listen less to the likes of Beethoven, Debussy, the sturdy Mr. E. Carter, these days. Birdsong will often do, and the ordinary kind, sparrows and robins. Today, neither the rain nor the robin seems willing to give up. It's an ordinary robin, the shapes of its song circular gestures, certainly not narrative. This, I suppose, is the kind of quiet ending Brahms chose for his Third Symphony, pastoral, resigned. Harold has probably discussed it with him. At this moment, perhaps, they are lighting cigars together.

Caught the . . . orchestra concert last night. They always play pretty & darned good, too. I always seem not to be in the mood for whatever they've chosen to program, however. Claude Frank yawned his way through the Beethoven 3ʳᵈ, even his mistakes were uninteresting. Smetana, Britten, Leonora #7 egad. . . .

What's odd is that I hear voices now, not often, or to the point of distraction, and they are Harold's voices, of course. Not the ones he heard, mind you—he would never tell me that awful secret—but his voice—forgive me for saying "voices," but I must, because they come from all the corners of the forty years of our friendship. And they don't come unbidden. I must always listen for a time before they come.

It is raining now softly, almost tenderly. Could this be the end of the drought?